I squatted over the body. The man's arms were held against his chest. Clutched in his left hand was the neck of a broken bourbon bottle. His eyes looked into mine, but they were motionless. There was no need to check for a pulse. I touched my chin to my chest and whispered his name. Only the corral's sullen silence and the patter of rain on my head and shoulders answered me.

"Damn. It's…" Boyd stood over me and gagged. Once he caught his breath, he commanded, "Give me my rifle. That horse needs killin'."

"Ella," I yelled above the storm. "Call my dad. It's Cody West, and he's dead." I also instructed her to back the horse trailer all the way down to the barn's open outer doors.

My heart pitched with anger. "Mr. Boyd, I'm taking custody of both horses until the cause of Cody's death is determined."

His hands shot out. He grabbed me by both wrists and yanked me up. "Determined? The hell you say. It's obvious that killer stomped Cody to death."

Lights…
Camera…Murder!

by

Loretta C. Rogers

A Doc Holliday Mystery, Book 3

Lights...Camera...Murder!

Cover Art by *Diana Carlile*

The Wild Rose Press, Inc.
PO Box 708
Adams Basin, NY 14410-0708
Visit us at www.thewildrosepress.com

Publishing History
First Edition, 2022
Trade Paperback ISBN 978-1-5092-4286-3
Digital ISBN 978-1-5092-4287-0

A Doc Holliday Mystery, Book 3
Published in the United States of America

"Very few of us are what we seem to be."
~Agatha Christie,
from *The Man in the Mist*

Chapter One

Enigma is a place frozen in time, a quaint town where nothing really changes. Today, however, was different. The atmosphere could only be described as like the old buildings were holding their breaths... waiting, but waiting for what?

It was past Sunday noon by the time the fire was contained. Exhausted and soot covered, I joined my grandmother at Patty's Sweets 'n' Eats, Enigma's local pastry shop and café. My godfather, Charlie Whitehorse, followed by Ella Sanders, my vet tech assistant, seated themselves at the table. Patty Sweet and a waitress filled mugs of coffee and set plates of assorted pastries in front of us.

Tanti Crow, mayor of Enigma and my feisty grandmother, said, "You're as worn out as the rest of us, Patty. Sit down and let the waitresses do their jobs."

Patty is my grandmother's best friend and the vice-mayor of Enigma. She heaved an exhausted sigh and plopped heavily in a chair. "I can't believe it. I just can't believe both buildings are nothing more than a pile of burnt rubble."

My grandmother dribbled water onto a napkin and placed it against her eyes. "Praise the Great Father Spirit that no one was in either building. I shudder to think how any of us would have made it out alive if we'd been trapped in that antiquated elevator."

A bell over the door dingled. We all turned to see who had entered. My dad, Sheriff Henry Holliday, hung his hat on a rack by the door. Holes pockmarked his tan shirt where hot ash had landed. He heaved a tired sigh when he joined us. A waitress rushed over with a mug of coffee. He thanked her.

"Any word on how the fire started?" I asked.

The fire had consumed the hundred-year-old community center, and enough of the city's government building to call it a total loss. Thankfully, Grandmother, Patty, Ella, and I had managed to save the four computers that contained valuable city files, and a few historical items.

Dad swallowed a healthy slug of coffee. "Floyd Alderman said he'd have an answer for me early next week."

Grandmother nearly choked on her donut. "The fire inspector, that Floyd? Henry, please don't tell me you suspect arson?"

Dad gave her one of his enduring looks. "It's routine, Tanti." He cast a warning glare around the table. "Don't go starting any unfounded rumors. Like I said, it's routine."

I jumped in to help Dad. Not that he needed my help. Just sayin'. "Everything in the building was as ancient as it was. There's no telling when the electrical wiring was last updated. I'll bet a dime to a donut that Mr. Alderman finds a charred rat or two with wire clamped between their teeth."

Dad smiled. "That's my Punk, always thinking logically. It's a known fact that both buildings have had rodent problems for years."

Uncle Charlie chimed in. "Hey, look at it like

this—we saved the town. Besides, now the council will have no excuses for not coughing up funds to rebuild."

Tanti sighed. "This doesn't bode well for Premier Entertainment Productions. If Joel and Barry Hermann think the town is unsafe, they might fold up their tents and take their money someplace else. Goodness knows Enigma can use all the revenue we can get. Especially now."

Patty sounded downcast. "Yes, and we've worked so hard to make a good impression on PEP. We're fortunate they chose our town over Louisville or Lexington, or even Elizabethtown."

"Don't worry, Grandmother. I'm sure the Mr. Hermanns have encountered much worse than a burnt-down building. After all, it's not like the buildings at the fairground were affected. I'm sure the fire didn't interrupt their filming schedule."

She looked so disheartened that I wrapped my hand around hers. "Neither you nor Patty need worry. All those late nights and early mornings you've put in to bring success to our town will pay off." I offered her my most empathetic smile. "Trust me."

Grandmother patted my arm. I added, "I have to do an inspection of the production company's animals tomorrow. If I hear any negative comments about our town, I'll be happy to set the naysayers straight. Besides, I've never seen so many tourists in my life. Think of the money they're spending."

Her dark eyes glistened with tears. "Always so positive. What on earth would I do without you?"

Charlie polished off another chocolate éclair. He wiped his mouth with a napkin. "Speaking of tourists, business at the saloon is booming, and I ain't complaining."

Ella seemed to be dozing in her chair. We were all in great need of rest and cool showers. I reached for another donut. I chomped on it and was in the process of licking the sugary tidbits from my lips when I felt as if I'd been stomped in the chest. Air wheezed from my lungs. It felt as if each heartbeat vibrated inside my ears. I remember clutching my chest. I don't remember moaning.

"Tullah...Punkin..." Dad's voice cut through my brain's misted fog. "Talk to me."

Somewhere, I thought I heard Grandmother say, "Shh. I think she's entered the spirit world."

I'm Tullah Crow Holliday, a doctor of veterinary medicine with secondary degrees in both human and animal forensics. I am licensed to practice in the state of Kentucky, operating an animal clinic in the small rural town of Enigma, where I have lived my entire twenty-nine years, not counting the years I attended the University of Georgia. And before you ask, yes, I do get kidded a lot about being someone's huckleberry, and yes, the infamous outlaw, Doc "John Henry" Holliday, is my ancestor on my father's side. By the way, it just so happens that my father, also named John Henry Holliday, is the sheriff of Enigma. I always bite down my irritation at the remarks. It wasn't until after my mother's tragic death that I began having some downright scary memory quirks.

I gasped and started coughing. Charlie, a stalwart man with threads of silver running through his long black ponytail, jumped up and pounded me on the back. I raised my hand. Before he could beat me to death with his powerful blows, I managed to choke out, "I'm okay."

Grandmother slid a glass of iced water in front of me. The water soothed my burning throat and helped wash down the remainder of the donut.

"What was it, Granddaughter? Another one of your visions?"

I was afraid to speak in case the effort set off another paroxysm of coughing. I sipped slowly. I had no explanation for what had just happened. Dad's eyes swiveled back to me.

I rasped out, "The answer is no…I didn't have a vision…and…" I searched for a plausible answer for my sudden attack. "It's all Patty's fault." I offered a sterling smile, hoping to soften my snotty retort. "If your donuts weren't so delicious, I wouldn't have overly stuffed my mouth and choked myself."

Patty grinned and rolled her eyes. "Perhaps a dose of castor oil will cure what ails you."

The mention of such a nasty-tasting concoction not only roiled my stomach but brought a genuine shudder.

Grandmother stretched and yawned. I took my cue from her. "I'm with you, Grandmother. Being routed out of bed in the wee hours of the morning is taking a toll on all of us. Thank goodness it's Sunday. Barring emergencies, I'm going home and straight to bed."

Ella pushed back her chair. "Sounds like a plan."

I hugged Dad, Charlie, Grandmother, and Patty. Even as I tried to casually stroll to the door, the constriction in my chest and throat grew, nearly strangling me.

Outside in the truck, Ella said, "I'll call the service and have them direct any emergencies to Dr. Cooper in Dixie County."

"Thanks, Ella. You remember Dr. Cooper is officially retiring at the end of July?"

"I heard your former assistant bought his practice."

"Cindi Redfern, yes. I'm happy for her."

"Are you afraid she might try to take some of your clients?"

I cast Ella a questioning look. "Not in the least. In fact, I offered Cindi a partnership. She handled all the small animals when she was here, while I took care of the large animal clinic."

"Wow, that sounds like the perfect setup. Do you know why she turned you down?"

I thought back about Earl Redfern, Cindi's father. The memory of his breaking into my house, the beating he gave me, and his threats to kill me cut into me like a wound that refused to heal. Thankfully, he was still in prison.

"Enigma holds more bad memories than good for Cindi. I believe she just needs a fresh start where people will know her as Dr. Redfern and not the daughter of a vicious drunk."

I passed the sign announcing my veterinary clinic and turned the truck down the winding lane that led to my house and animal hospital. There is something about horses and cattle grazing in waist-high grass that eases the soul.

I drove under the carport and shut off the ignition. The late afternoon, tempered by July's heat, greeted us as we stepped from the vehicle. River, my black Lab, and Rascal, my gray teacup donkey, and Ella's two Jack Russell terriers, Pogo and Ozzie, swamped us with happy attention.

No words were needed as Ella and her pups trotted

toward the silver travel trailer she calls home. My pets followed me inside as I unlocked the kitchen door. I usually open the doggie door for River and Rascal to come and go as they please. Since they had been out all morning, I decided not to open the door. Instead, I trudged upstairs, removing my shirt as I went. I was praying the phone wouldn't ring. Deciding to forego a shower, I managed to shuck the rest of my clothes, pull on my oversized T-shirt, and crawl into bed before sleep hit me.

It was past midnight, some lonely, small hour of the morning, when I awoke drenched in sweat. Moonlight streamed between the closed curtains. I squeezed my eyes shut. Even my eyelids were sweating. My dream had been one big close-up of a gaping hole in a man's bloodied chest, his eyes wide and staring.

I blew my breath out and fought against the breathless panic that threatened to overtake me. River placed his large paws on the edge of the bed and whined. Rascal expelled one of his little snuffling brays.

I patted their heads. "It's okay. I'm okay. Go back to sleep." I rolled out of bed and crossed to the window. Closing my eyes, I pressed my forehead to the cool glass. Something was going to happen. My stomach cramped at the thought.

A little voice inside my head whispered, *He's dead.*

Chapter Two

Ella squealed. "Cody West! I can't believe I might get to see him in person. Oh, Tullah, he's so handsome. You should have seen him in *Ride Hard to Sundown.* The man can truly sit a horse."

I kept my eyes on the road as I drove toward the fairgrounds where PEP had set up their production company. "I can honestly say that I've never seen a Cody West movie."

She gasped and grabbed her chest as if stricken. "Tullah, you have to stop living under a rock. You've *never* seen a Cody West movie? Why…why…that's almost sacrilege."

Be that as it may, my mind was busy being thankful for the truck's air conditioner. Nothing outside seemed to move. Huge cumulus clouds bobbed along in an ocean of blue as the morning sun rose higher and the day got hotter. In fact, the asphalt road already shimmered like water in the heat.

I smiled at my assistant. "If it makes you feel any better, I have watched several Audie Murphy, Jimmy Stewart, and Randolph Scott westerns."

She flashed me an incredulous frown. "Who are they?"

"Hah. Now who's living under a rock?" I wheeled into the entrance that led to the livestock pens. The area where ranchers usually parked their stock trailers was filled with a sea of travel trailers and motor homes. The multitude of homes on wheels blocked the route I needed to take to the large barn and outside corrals.

I stopped at a ticket booth, where a railroad-type crossarm blocked my way.

Ella said, "That's never been there before."

A man in his late twenties, his spiked black hair with green tips reminding me of a chia pet, leaned out of the booth. "You can't go back here unless you have official PEP ID."

"I'm Doctor Holliday. I'm here to inspect the horses and cattle to make sure they're—"

"Yeah, yeah." He sneered. "You're Doc Holliday and I'm Wyatt Earp, and who is she, Annie Oakley? Show me your *official* PEP ID, and I'll let you pass."

I gritted my teeth to keep from telling this idiot to jerk off. "Mr. Hank Boyd is expecting me."

"Uh-huh, and Little Red Riding Hood is expecting me. C'mon, lady, g'me a break. I've heard every excuse in the world from women who either want to slobber all over the *infamous* Cody West or flash their boobs around hoping to get a bit part in one of his pictures."

I looked at his name tag. "Mr. Apollo, I see that you have a cellphone. Call Mr. Boyd, and he'll vouch for me."

When he hesitated, I cocked an eyebrow and pierced him with my best *I'm not in the mood* look. "Either contact Mr. Boyd, or let me through." I revved the truck's engine. "Because if you don't, I'll make my own opening."

He groused while he punched his phone and made the call. "Okay…yeah…yeah. Just doing my job." He disconnected and scowled at me. "Some days I'd like to take this job and shove it where there ain't no sunshine. It orta be the high and mighty West standing out here in the scalding heat and me with the star over my door."

Ella said, "Cody is a talented actor. He's kind and handsome and loves horses."

Apollo mimicked jamming his finger down his throat and gagging. "What you see on screen is called acting! West is about as phony as a two-dollar bill."

Spittle spewed from his mouth. I drew back. "There's no need to shout, Mr. Apollo."

It was almost as if Frankie Apollo realized he had talked out of turn. He wasn't a handsome man, but neither was he ugly. A bit pudgy around the waist, nothing a little exercise wouldn't cure. I wondered why he resented PEP's A-list cowboy star.

"Sorry. I didn't mean to get so riled up."

"I take it you're not part of Mr. West's fan club."

He ignored my comment and said, "Hank says you're legit. Holliday Veterinary Clinic—says so right there on your truck." He emitted a little chuckle. "I should've noticed before shooting off my mouth. Wait just a minute."

He pulled something from a shelf and bent to whatever he was doing. In a couple of minutes, he handed out two fluorescent orange lanyards, both not only imprinted "PEP" but with our names written on the tags, followed by his signature. "Wear these anytime you're on the premises, and no one will give you a second notice." He hesitated. "Sometimes I get teased about my name—Apollo. I'm not exactly a Greek god. Hope you won't mention this to my uncles."

"Your uncles?"

"Yeah, Joel and Barry. My mother is their sister.

She keeps bugging me about when am I gonna be in a movie. I tell her to bug her brothers, not me." He offered a lopsided smile. "Anyhow, there might not be enough room to maneuver your truck close to the barn." He pointed. "Park over there, and it's just a short walk through trailer city. And Ella, you might get to see Cody. He's in a fancy maroon-and-cream RV, the one with the gold star next to his name on the door."

Frankie Apollo stepped out of the booth, lifted the crossarm, and waved us through. I knew my way around the stockyards enough to know I'd be better off parking and walking in than risk sideswiping one of the million-dollar homes on wheels.

Ella and I collected the medical bags loaded with equipment we needed to draw blood from the horses to test for equine encephalitis and from the cattle for the Bangs disease testing. It's not that I didn't trust Mr. Hank Boyd, PEP's top wrangler. It's more like my motto is never trust paperwork that's too easily altered. I'd seen altered paperwork too many times from various racetrack officials.

"Tullah, would you take a picture of me standing in front of Cody's motorhome? I mean, even if I don't get to see him in person, I'll at least have a memento."

"Sure, why not."

"How much do you think one of these costs? I'd love to take a peek inside."

I loosed a whistle. "I have no idea. Probably more than I'll make in several lifetimes."

As we approached a blue-and-gray RV, we heard a woman shouting. At first we couldn't make out what she was saying. When we got closer, we could see the shades were drawn and the door was closed, but we heard a man say, "Calm down, Nikki. I'll handle it."

The woman's voice replied, "You don't get it, Lou. I dread the love scenes. Cody seems to think I enjoy having his tongue jammed down my throat. His mouth always tastes like stale whiskey, and his breath is foul enough to curl my toenails."

"I hear you. I do all the stunts, take the bruises and broken bones, and Cody gets all the glory. I hate the way he's always giving me advice about how to ride or shoot, or take a fall. He'd cry if he broke one of his manicured fingernails. There are times when I'd really like to twist his scrawny neck until it snapped."

The woman named Nikki laughed. "What a joke. If people only knew his real name is Stanley Eisenbarth! But oh, no, he's Cody West. What if people knew he uses women and then throws them away like trash? What if they knew he was a closet alcoholic?"

"You can always quit, Nikki."

Bitterness laced her voice. "You know I can't, and you know why."

"Then go to either Joel or Barry."

"Are you crazy? I'd ruin my career forever."

There was a tense silence. I felt terrible eavesdropping. Just as I motioned to Ella for us to leave, the woman said, "Maybe I should tell Miss Prissy Pants that Cody is using her like he used me. There are nights when all I dream about is how to kill Mr. Cody West."

The door opened. Ella and I quickly jumped behind the motor coach. A tall man wearing tan chinos, a tan shirt, black leather vest, and western boots with spurs stepped to the ground. He turned back and said, "Stop worrying, hon. Like I said, I'll take care of it."

I think we held our breaths until we were sure the coast was clear. I motioned for Ella to follow me. "We'll casually walk past the door. If the woman opens it, we'll tell her the truth, that we're here to test the animals."

Ella nodded. The name next to a large gold star stated Dominique Dupont. Ella lifted her cellphone camera and clicked. We then hustled past. When we were well enough away, she whispered, "The man called her Nikki. I wonder who was inside."

Although I didn't see his face, there was something familiar about the man. My heart thudded against my chest. For a moment it felt as if I might faint. I blamed it on the heat. "I don't know and don't care. Let's do what we came for and get back to the clinic."

As we approached the main barn, a man sporting a thick mustache and wearing a white cowboy hat met us. "Dr. Holliday, I'm Hank Boyd. I'm sorry you had a bit of trouble with Frankie Apollo."

"It's no biggie. He was just doing his job."

"Well, Frankie can be a bit of a nuisance at times."

Ella said, "He sure isn't a fan of Cody West."

"No, ma'am." He said it in a way that meant *drop the subject.* "Starlight, that's Cody's horse, is in here along with the other stunt horses. The cattle are in the large corral at the other end of the barn."

We followed Mr. Boyd into the barn. It took a moment for my eyes to adjust to the dim interior. A magnificent golden head stretched its neck over the stall door and whinnied. I ran my hand down the palomino's neck and spoke to him before I lifted the lead rope off its hook and snapped it to the halter's O-ring. Hank Boyd opened the door, and I led the horse out.

13

"Um, are you sure this is the horse Mr. West rides in the movies?"

"Of course I'm sure. Why do you ask?"

I glanced at Ella, who was preparing to draw a vial of blood from Starlight's neck. "According to my assistant, Mr. West rides a stallion." I cocked an eyebrow. "This is a gelding."

"Oh, that." He chuckled. "Statistics show that most moviegoers don't know the difference between a stallion and a gelding. Besides, Mr. Cantrell prefers geldings, says they're easier to handle."

"Mr. Cantrell?"

"Yep, Lou Cantrell. He's Cody's stand-in. Does all the stunts, takes the falls, that sort of thing."

Ah, so that's who was in the motorhome with Nikki what's her name. I opened Starlight's mouth and checked his teeth, then ran my hands down his legs and checked all four hooves. "Rubber shoes. I assume this is to accommodate the severe arthritis in his legs."

Hank Boyd nodded. "Yep, poor guy, I hate it when Lou has to make him rear."

I straightened. "Starlight is up in years. Twenty-eight is old for a stunt horse."

Boyd grinned. "You know your stuff, Doc. As a matter of fact, just like we use stunt people for the actors, we have stand-ins for Starlight."

"Uh, Mr. Boyd?" Ella peered over the palomino's back. "What did you mean when you said Cantrell prefers geldings? Doesn't Cody do all of his own riding?"

This time Boyd guffawed. "Hardly. Cody claims to be allergic to horses. Truth be known, he's petrified of them."

The surprised look on Ella's face was priceless. She said, "But I've watched every one of his movies, and he always springs into the saddle, has Starlight rear up, and then gallops off to catch the bad guys."

Hank Boyd offered Ella a kindly smile. "Ma'am, I'm truly sorry to have to burst your bubble. What you see is Cody with his foot in the stirrup and his hands on the saddle horn. What you don't see is when the cameras stop rolling and Cody's stunt double is called in. I tell you what—Cody and Lou are shooting a fight scene tomorrow morning. Barbara Nettles is the assistant director on this shoot. I'll let her know the two of you are my VIP guests. She'll make sure you're seated close enough to catch all the action. Then, Miss Ella, you'll see what I'm talking about."

A series of loud whinnies and heavy hoof thuds against a wall drew our attention. Hank Boyd said, "That would be Spitfire. He's our newest acquisition." He lifted an eyebrow and grinned. "And a stallion."

We strolled down the wide aisle to the stall. Hank advised us to stand back. "He's a biter. Actually reared and tried to stomp one of the stable girls when she opened the stall door to put feed in his bucket."

"Why would you purchase such a volatile animal?"

Hank shrugged. "You've seen the other palominos. They're as close as we've been able to come for Starlight lookalikes, but they just don't match his spirit or camera sense. When I saw Spitfire at an auction, I nearly swallowed my teeth. It's like the two of them were cloned. Thing is, he's crazy wild."

I reached out my hand, palm up, and spoke to the young stallion in Cherokee. His eyes were round and fierce with mistrust. I continued to whisper until he

15

relented and stretched his neck to lip the tips of my fingers. I rubbed down his golden neck and continued whispering to him. The rage inside him eased enough for me to open his mouth and check his teeth.

"I'd put him about two years old. Do you plan to geld him?"

When Hank didn't answer, I said, "Mr. Boyd?"

"Oh, yeah, sure. I've never seen anything like that. We had to tranquilize him just to get him loaded into the trailer and then inside the stall. But, yeah, I'd be obliged to have you take care of the castration."

I checked my calendar and set a date and time that I would arrive with my equipment. I figured it was easier for me to come to the horse than to risk anyone getting hurt trying to load and transport Spitfire to my clinic.

Hank tipped his hat and said he needed to meet with Sam Jessup, the senior director. We thanked him for the VIP privileges and went about collecting samples of blood from all the animals.

When we'd finished and were strolling back to the truck, Ella said, "Wow, those animals sure do get treated like royalty."

"That's for sure. I'm glad there's no sign of abuse. It'd break Grandmother's heart if I had to shut down production and call in Animal Services. I hope all the bloodwork comes back negative."

We deliberately skirted away from where my truck was parked. Ella insisted on finding Cody's motorhome. Like a happy child, she skipped forward. "There it is."

And there it was. I swear that maroon-and-cream coach didn't have a speck of dust on it. The star above his name shone like new money. Ella had just lifted her phone to focus the camera when we heard moans and gagging.

"Should we knock on the door to see if he's okay?"

When I hesitated, she said, "Tullah, you're a doctor. Maybe he's sick."

Then a woman's voice scolded, "Cody, you're drunk. Come on, drink some coffee. We need to rehearse our lines."

"Go 'way!" The words were slurred. "I'll know my lines. Now get the hell out!"

"Have it your way. It's only a matter of time before—"

We heard the door click. Then Cody yelled, "No, wait. Bring me another bottle, and my pills."

I grabbed Ella by the arm. "This is none of our business. Let's get out of here."

Once the medical equipment was secured, we stepped inside the truck, and I hit the ignition. Frankie Apollo saw us coming and left the booth to lift the crossbar for us to leave the stockyard. We returned his wave and kept driving.

Ella wasn't her usual chatty self. I said, "You're awfully quiet."

"Disappointed, I guess, to learn that my cowboy hero is really a fake."

"You're a smart young woman, Ella. You know movies are fiction."

"I know. It's all playacting. But it's kinda nice living in a fantasy world where the hero is a cut above other men. What woman doesn't want to fall in love with a knight in shining armor or a handsome cowboy wearing a white hat and riding a golden palomino?"

She heaved a heavy sigh.

"Cheer up. Let's swing by the Whitehorse Saloon and indulge in one of Charlie's special hamburgers." I grinned and waggled my eyebrows. "My treat. It's Monday, and I'll bet he's ordered chocolate eclairs from Patty's Sweets 'n' Eats."

"If you're trying to bribe me into feeling better, it's working." She smiled even though it was a bit limp.

While I drove, Ella googled something on her phone. "Dominique Dupont's real name is Nikki Lewiki, and it's true, Cody's real name *is* Stanley Eisenbarth." She slipped the phone into her shirt pocket. "I'm completely bummed."

I pulled into the saloon's parking lot. "Poor Nikki Lewiki. Can you imagine the ribbing she must have gotten in school? And Eisenbarth—what can I say? I'd change my name too."

She looked at me and grinned. "No, you wouldn't…Doc HOLLIDAY!"

We laughed as we strolled through the doors of my godfather's saloon.

Chapter Three

The saloon was usually quiet until dark-thirty. With the movie production company in town, today like most days since PEP's arrival saw the Whitehorse filled with noisy tourists. Charlie's new waitress, Sally Davenport, balanced a tray of drinks as she expertly wove between tables. I watched her set the frosted mugs of beer in front of the customers. She used the back of her hand to swipe a wayward strand of blonde hair from her face.

A woman in her mid-thirties, and as Charlie would say, not hard on the eyes, Sally was new to Engima. She had used the last of her money to drive from New York to Enigma only to discover the big part her agent had promised in Cody's new movie was not the leading lady but rather a one-liner as a saloon girl. Well, she's a saloon girl, all right. Since Flo's retirement and with the influx of people, Sally was in the right place at the right time to get a job.

"Gosh, Tullah, it doesn't look like there's any places to sit. People are even standing at the bar," Ella commented.

I scanned the large room. Someone called my name. "Look, there's my dad." We threaded our way to Dad's favorite booth, the one where he can observe most of the action without being seen.

"Where's Charlie?"

Dad answered, "Helping in the kitchen."

"Looks like he needs to hire more help."

Dad nodded his agreement. "With one waitress, it may be a while before you get waited on. She hasn't gotten around to taking my order yet."

I glanced around. "I guess she doesn't know the sheriff gets priority."

Dad's phone chirped. "Go ahead, Tiny." He listened, then said to Ella and me, "Catch you girls later. Chamberlin Harris says he just discovered two of his thoroughbreds missing. Tiny found truck and trailer tracks in the back pasture."

I gasped. "Who in their right mind would steal two prize horses, and in broad daylight?"

When Sally Davenport hustled over to another table, I said, "Ella, will you take a raincheck on the hamburger? It doesn't look like we'll get waited on anytime soon."

"What about Patty's? It's hot, and I could go for one of Patty's chocolate milkshakes and a sandwich."

We spotted Dad at his 4-Runner, waved goodbye, and followed him toward town. I honked my horn when we pulled in front of Sweets 'n' Eats Café. This place was bustling too, but fortunately Grandmother called to us. As soon as we were seated, Patty in her signature pink apron rushed over to our table with order pad and pen in hand. She lamented, "I'm thankful for the business, but my dogs are barking and my back is killing me. I'm getting too old for this."

Grandmother said, "Hire another waitress for the café. You can always supervise or run the pastry end of the business."

Patty chuffed at Grandmother's comment, then

turned her attention to us. Ella and I placed our order. By the time our food arrived, the crowd had thinned out, and Patty joined us. She sighed when she sat. "So what's new with you girls?"

Ella piped up about our encounter with Spitfire. "I swear, Tullah is the ultimate horse whisperer. It seems she has a magical way with all animals."

I don't like having such attention, and quickly changed the subject. "How did it go this morning, Grandmother? Did you and Patty get selected as movie extras?"

Grandmother harrumphed. "There must have been three hundred people standing in line. Patty and I decided we had too much to do besides standing in the hot sun when our chances of getting chosen were slim to none."

Patty chimed in. "But we did get something just as exhilarating. Because Tanti is the mayor and I'm the vice mayor, we were given VIP passes to watch Cody West and the other actors shoot a barroom scene tomorrow."

Ella and I exchanged smiles. I said, "Then we can all ride together, because Hank Boyd, PEP's top wrangler, invited us."

Grandmother clasped her hands together. "This is so exciting! Just think, up close and personal with movie stars. If you'll excuse me, I need to work on the next edition of the *Enigma Bulletin*."

We finished our lunch and ordered iced teas to go. Grandmother said she and Patty would meet us at the studio. "There's no need for you to drive all the way into town, then all the way to the fairgrounds, then all the way back to town to bring us home. Besides, there's always the possibility one of your clients could call with an emergency. We'd be stranded."

Her frown eased into a smile when I hugged her. "You're always so logical, Grandmother."

We waved our goodbyes. On the drive back to the clinic, my phone rang. "Dr. Holliday, how may I help you?"

A panicked voice said, "Doc, this is Stu Dodd. I'm sittin' in front of your clinic. Where are you?"

"I'm five minutes away. What's up, Mr. Dodd?"

"It's Mr. Puggles, my French Bulldog. He's frothing at the mouth. I checked him over and don't think he's been snake bit."

I pulled next to Dodd's truck. Ella jumped out and said, "I'll open the door and get the surgery ready."

"Bring the gurney instead." I grabbed my medical bag and rushed to the lethargic, salivating dog. Before I could remove my stethoscope, he started convulsing.

"Quick, let's get him inside. He's suffering from a heat stroke." The dog was heavy. It took all my strength and Ella's help, but we managed to get him on the gurney and wheeled inside the surgery.

We left the dog on the gurney and immediately applied cool, wet cloths to the overweight bulldog. After we had brought Mr. Puggles' temperature to normal and I was satisfied he was resting easily, I advised Mr. Dodd to keep the dog cool and well hydrated, and not to hesitate to call me.

"I don't know how to thank you, Doc. He was my wife's dog, and…" Stu Dodd was in his eighties and a widower. His voice broke with emotion. "Mr. Puggles is all I have left. I surely do appreciate your saving him."

My heart broke a little. The bulldog was overweight and elderly. I figured he might have another year left before crossing the rainbow bridge. I didn't have the heart to tell Mr. Dodd.

The rest of the afternoon was crazy busy. Appointments were scheduled back to back. I had to refer an emergency call to Dr. Cooper in Dixie County.

By the time we locked the clinic, fed all the animals, and tended the horses, I think Ella and I were both too tired to walk the short distance to our respective dwellings. Instead, I opened the small refrigerator that I keep in the clinic and grabbed a cola for both of us. We sank into the waiting room chairs.

I noted that Ella wasn't her usual chatty self. Maybe she was too tired to talk. Either way, I didn't feel like engaging in meaningless conversation. I drew a long, cold, and refreshing gulp of cola.

"Tullah, I know bulldogs are considered a brachycephalic breed, but how did you specifically know to treat him for heat stroke?"

"Well, his drool was thicker and stickier than normal, and his gums were purple, which denotes dehydration, plus the usual dry nose and excessive heavy panting."

Ella rolled the cold cola can across her forehead. "He wouldn't have survived without your expertise."

I assured her that with time and experience she would also be alert to such symptoms. I finished my drink and tossed the can in the recycle bin.

"Are you excited about tomorrow, Tullah?"

Every now and then a sliver of a dark thought tries to slip in. I shoved it away. I didn't want to dampen Ella's excitement. "I'm sure it'll be an interesting day."

"I'll bet Tanti and Patty are excited."

"I'm sure."

We said our goodnights and walked outside. I had barely reached the carport when River let out a series of serious barks. I peered into the gloom. Shivers chilled me.

After a refreshing shower and a quick dinner of leftover macaroni and cheese, I climbed into bed and opened my newest mystery novel, *Murder in the Mist*. I turned to the page where the heroine, Laura Friday, had fallen into a grave and landed on top of a skeleton. I don't remember falling asleep. I dreamed. Mother was pushing me in a swing. We were laughing. I pretended I was a bird soaring high in the sky.

The dream changed.

Horses rearing... gnashing teeth... long-necked palominos with demon eyes, stretching their necks toward each other... fire... licking flames... rats... lots of rats... a man... he turns to me... the sun is in my eyes... I can't see his face... the dust on his chest is stained red... I wipe my hands on my jeans... Tears stain my mother's face... she fades away... my skinny arms are shivering... I call to her.

River's whines awakened me as he licked my face. It took a moment to regain my equilibrium. I saw by the clock that it was seven thirty.

Somehow, I knew today was not going to be fun.

Chapter Four

I turned the water on full force and let it get good and steamy before stepping into the shower. My first conscious thought was about the dream. What did it mean? Was it an omen? The next thought, did my life have any meaning?

For all practical purposes, I had a neat and tidy life in a messy world. I was a successful veterinarian; I owned my own practice. I had a loving father and a doting grandmother. I had experienced scary quirks of memory and helped my dad solve several crimes. In the meantime, I could have a small pride in myself, although I don't consider myself a prideful person.

I went through the tedious routine of drying my mass of hair, pulled on a pair of jeans and a new blue shirt. I padded downstairs in my socks and brewed a cup of coffee. Have I mentioned that I love the new insta-cup brewer that Grandmother gave me last Christmas?

I had plenty of time before Ella and I left for the movie set. I settled in my recliner and opened my laptop to read Grandmother's online newspaper article. "Town Set Ablaze," read the headline. A picture of my dad and Charlie accompanied the report. I scanned the article quickly. It was necessarily short and didn't hint at the possibility of arson. I knew Dad had requested that piece of information be withheld until otherwise proven. However, it would be all over Enigma soon, I was sure.

I thought about the dream and my mother. It was four years since her brutal murder. I burst into tears and slopped coffee all down the front of my new blue shirt. I had barely changed into a clean shirt when Ella rapped on the kitchen door. She must have sensed that I wasn't in the mood for her usual morning exuberance and forewent her normal chatter. As I walked slowly out to my truck, I was still mulling over the dream.

"You're awfully quiet, Tullah. Are you all right this morning?"

"Yes," I said, and I meant it.

We drove the remaining distance to the fairgrounds in silence. As usual, the parking lot was filled with vehicles sporting out-of-state tags. Vendors outside the entrance gate had set up kiosks selling everything from autographed photos of famous actors to T-shirts with famous actors' quotes printed across the front.

I parked. We wended our way to the entrance gate. The security guard offered a genuine smile. "Doc Holliday and Ella, remember me?"

"Good morning, Mr. Apollo," Ella and I chimed.

"Hey, call me Frankie. No hard feelings 'bout yesterday, I hope."

I offered my best grin. "All forgotten."

"I see you're wearing your lanyards."

I had a sudden flood of nervous energy as I held my neon orange ID forward. "We're supposed to meet Barbara Nettles, the assistant director. Can you direct us to the exact shooting location?"

"I can do better than that. Hang on for a second." Frankie spoke into a walkie-talkie. A young woman wearing a security guard uniform appeared driving a golf cart. "Here ya go, Frankie."

He stepped out of the booth and held his hand forward. "Your carriage awaits, ladies, and I'm your personal driver. Hank told me to keep a watch out for you."

He chatted a mile a minute as he expertly wove through pockets of people. "I'll be flying back to New York on Sunday. Got a part in the Broadway musical *Jersey Boys.*"

Ella gushed, "Gosh, you sing?"

"Yep, play the piano, guitar, and violin, too. Guess graduating from Julliard is finally paying off. At least my mother's happy, and I think my uncles are glad to have me out of their hair."

I thought he sounded a bit disappointed. "Congratulations, Frankie. I'm sure it won't be long before you're on the front page of all the movie magazines."

"It's nice of you to say so, and I really do apologize for being so rude yesterday."

He parked in front of the agricultural building that's generally used for showing 4-H art work, horticulture, and junior cooking contests, among other events. Today a sign designated the building as set number twenty-three, with a large sign printed in bold red letters: Closed Set!

Frankie removed his cellphone and punched in numbers. He said, "Ms. Nettles, Hank Boyd's guests have arrived."

While we waited for someone to open the locked door, Frankie handed us a packet of papers. "I thought you might like a copy of these. They're call sheets.

Usually only the actors and pertinent staff get 'em. It has today's schedule on it." He pointed. "As you can see, it lists each member of the cast, a breakdown of their scenes, and the exact time they're to be on set. Anyhow, it makes the day go smoother."

We wished Frankie good luck on his Broadway debut. He waved goodbye and drove off in the golf cart. A stocky woman with pink hair and wearing black owl-round glasses greeted us. The moment I walked through the open door, I felt as if I'd stepped back in time. The entire auditorium had been transformed into an 1800s American western saloon.

"I'm Gloria Farnham, Ms. Nettles' assistant." She directed us to follow her. "There are a few rules you need to follow." She ticked off the instructions as if she'd repeated them numerous times. "Turn off your phone or place it on vibrate. Absolutely no talking, not even a whisper. Once filming begins, remain seated, even if you need to use the bathroom." She pierced us with a cocked eyebrow that almost dared us to defy her. "Do not approach the actors. Do not take pictures of them or video the shoot. The actors are in character and are not to be distracted, and you have about twenty minutes to wander around the set. Be careful, as you can see there is a multitude of equipment and cables." She drew a breath. "Any questions?"

Before either Ella or I could respond, Ms. Farnham said, "Good." She pointed to a dimly lit back corner. "Help yourselves to refreshments, but be finished before shooting begins." With that she turned on her heel and left.

I looked at Ella, who merely shook her head in dismay. "C'mon," I said, and headed to the refreshment

28

table.

Ella grimaced. "She'd make a perfect drill sergeant."

"Welcome to my refreshment table. What's your pleasure?"

"I'll have a chocolate glazed donut and coffee, black." I reached for my wallet.

"Oh, no charge. We keep refreshments for all the staff on shoot days." She huffed a sigh. "Sure keeps me busy when there're multiple shoots. I have to pack up my cart and rush to the next set, then set up—but I'm not complaining." She held out the cup of coffee. "By the way, my name is Kellyanne Simpson, famously known as 'the refreshment lady.' Sometimes I think no one really knows my name."

"Dr. Tullah Holliday, and Ella Sanders, my assistant. We're guests of Hank Boyd."

"Yep," Ella chimed in. "I'm really excited to see Cody West in action."

I thought I detected a slight hint of disgust with the way Kellyanne quirked her lip upward.

A young man walked over and handed Kellyanne a tall sports bottle. "Mr. Jessup's usual."

She filled the bottle with crushed ice, squeezed two lemon slices, and then filled it with expensive bottled water. She capped the container and handed it back to the man. "That's Jered. He's Sam Jessup's gofer."

"Sam Jessup?" I asked.

"You know, the executive director."

We thanked Kellyanne and meandered to the chairs. Remembering Gloria Farnham's warning, I cringed when my phone rang. "Hi, Grandmother, I thought you'd be here by now."

"You're not going to believe this." Tanti's voice sounded troubled. "There was a small fire in the café's kitchen. Patty is beside herself."

"Do you need us? Was Patty hurt? Where's Dad?"

"Slow down, Tullah. No one was hurt. The fire department has everything under control. I'm just letting you know that Patty and I won't make it to the movie set. We're both bummed, of course, but I'm staying to help her clean up."

"We'll be right there."

"No, you won't! Stay and enjoy yourselves." Grandmother hesitated and then with a little chuckle said, "But you could bring us a souvenir on your way home."

I promised. I explained to Ella about the fire. "I hope two fires just days apart is a coincidence."

"Don't overthink it, Tullah. Maybe one of the employees simply forgot to turn off a stove or left a dishrag too close to a burner."

Her logic made sense even if I didn't entirely agree with her.

A door slammed. I turned to look. A woman wearing a red-and-black corseted dress, black fishnet stockings, and a red-and-black feathered boa draped around her shoulders entered the room. She pulled a chair from one of the tables and sat.

Ella and I grinned at each other. The saloon girl was being played by none other than Sally Davenport, Charlie's new waitress. She looked our way, smiled, and gave a little wave.

We returned the greeting. I glanced down at the call sheet to see that she was playing the part of Belle, the saloon girl.

Other actors followed. It didn't take long before the room filled with a hum of frenetic energy. Ella tapped my arm and pointed. She mouthed, "That's Cody."

Because his tan felt hat was pulled down over his eyes, it was difficult to see the actor's face. What was evident was that he had more stumble than swagger when he crossed the room to push through the saloon doors.

Cameramen situated themselves behind large cameras set at different angles. A woman seated in a chair labeled Assistant Director, yelled, "Quiet on set." She yelled again, "Roll sound."

A camera operator responded, "Rolling."

At this point, a tall slender guy holding a clapboard with two sticks that resembled an open-mouthed PacMan wearing black-and-white lipstick walked out in front of the camera. He yelled, "Scene eighty-two, take one." Then he clapped the sticks firmly together to make a noise.

When he moved off camera, Sam Jessup, the primary director, raised his hand and called, "Action."

Cody was playing himself. José Pergola was playing the part of Cody's archenemy, Waco Bravo.

Cody pushed through the saloon doors. He hitched the gun belt at his waist and stepped forward. He scowled at a man's back. "Heard you had a score to settle with me, Waco."

Dressed in all black and propped against the bar, Waco Bravo twisted his top lip into a snarl as he slowly but deliberately turned and tipped back his black hat. He whipped a knife from the scabbard at his waist and pointed the tip at a jagged scar that marred his face. The blade glinted when he held it toward Cody.

Waco spoke with a raspy growl. "I came a thousand miles to kill you. I'm not gonna rush it. I'm gonna take my time and enjoy carving you into little pieces."

Cody responded, "It's..." He shifted slightly to look off camera.

A prompter held up a large white cue card. For a moment, I thought Cody might collapse. He definitely looked a bit peaked, maybe even hung over.

Cody picked up his line. "It's bad enough to have to kill a man, without having to listen to all of his stupid talk first."

Waco Bravo lunged forward.

Belle screamed, "Look out, Cody!"

Sally had had only one line, and I thought she played it convincingly. I held my breath. Ella gripped my arm. The two actors grappled into a bear hug and stumbled toward the stairs leading upward to the saloon's second level.

Sam Jessup yelled, "Cut! Cue stuntmen."

Cody and José separated and went to stand out of camera view. I was surprised when Cody disappeared around a faux wall. From all I'd read, not even A-list actors were allowed to leave the set, not for any reason, unless the director was happy with the end of the scene and called "Cut" without anything further.

Lou Cantrell and another stunt man entered and immediately mimicked the bear hug hold. Jessup yelled, "Action."

I glanced down at the call sheet to see the other stunt man was Mac Harris. With their hats pulled low and faces out of view, it was as Hank Boyd had said— difficult to tell Lou Cantrell from Cody West.

A brawl so convincing ensued that my body tensed and my breath hung in my throat. I glanced to see Ella on the edge of her chair. We watched the two men battle up the stairs and down the hallway, with Mac Harris forcing Lou Cantrell over the banister. For a split second the two men disappeared from view.

Some vague memory pressed against my brain, wanting out. Had it been part of my dream? Breath hung in my throat.

A gunshot boomed. My eyes shot upward. That little voice inside my head said, *He's dead.*

Sam Jessup yelled, "Cut! Cut! Who the hell ordered a gunshot?"

I barely remembered leaving my chair and rushing to where Lou Cantrell lay face down on an air mattress that had been placed earlier to catch his fall.

Ella whispered a loud warning, "Tullah, you can't be on the set. It's part of the act."

I knelt beside the body. Sam Jessup scowled at me. "Who the hell are you?" He looked around and demanded, "Somebody get her off my set."

Jessup tried to shove me aside. I snapped back. "He's dead." Don't ask me how I knew. I just knew. "Help me roll him over."

Chapter Five

Jessup merely gawped like I was a crazy woman. I rolled Lou over onto his back. His eyes were wide as if still in shock.

I put my fingers against his neck. No pulse, of course. Lou Cantrell was really dead.

Jessup cajoled. "Convincing, Lou, good job as usual, but you can get up now."

Barbara Nettles bent on her knees. She screamed—short, surprised, agonized. Blood oozed up, bright red, spreading easily across Lou's tan vest as if pleased to be released.

José Pergola was behind me in an instant. He said, "What's wrong?"

A voice called, "Help." We all looked up to see Mac Harris leaning over the railing. He held a hand to the back of his head. His voice was reedy when he spoke. "Somebody clobbered me on the back of the head. I think I need a doctor."

He gripped the railing and stumbled toward the stairs. At the top landing, his knees buckled. Sally Davenport raced to help him before he tumbled to the floor.

I grabbed my phone and punched Dad's emergency number. He answered in an instant. "What is it, Punkin?"

"There's been an accident, Dad. One of the

stuntmen is dead, and another one injured. Only, I don't think the death was an accident. I'll fill you in when you get here."

"You know what to do?"

"Yes, sir, secure the scene."

"Tiny and I'll be there asap."

"We need an ambulance and maybe Charlie, too. There're too many people for you and Tiny to process."

"On it!"

I thought fast, and grabbed Sam Jessup by the shoulders and spoke rapidly, not allowing the arrogant director to interrupt. "My name is Tullah Holliday, I'm a doctor." I deliberately omitted that I was a veterinarian. "My father is sheriff of Enigma. He and his deputy are on the way with an ambulance. I need your help in securing the scene."

Jessup dusted his fingers together. He stood as if lost in thought. "I-I don't have a script for this."

"Mr. Jessup, with your permission, I'll—" He nodded, looking almost relieved to let me handle the situation.

I interrupted the chatter. "Uh…people?…folks, may I have your attention, please?"

Voices stilled.

I said, with no particular emphasis, "There's been an unfortunate accident. Until Sheriff Holliday and Deputy Goodbody arrive, I'm asking you to all stay in this room for a little while."

Ella had removed a horse blanket used as a saloon prop and covered Lou's face and upper body. I gave her an appreciative smile.

One of the male actors rushed to Mac and helped Sally steer him into a chair. At this moment, I regretted not having my medical bag. My mind was firing in all directions as I approached the injured man. "My name is Tullah. I'm a doctor—well, actually a veterinarian. Mind if I take a look?"

"Mac Harris, Doc. I'm not sure what just happened." He was breathing hard and seemed to be shaking—out of shock, I imagined. His curly blond hair was matted with rusty red blood.

"That's quite a goose egg you have. Did you see who hit you?" I called for Ella to make up an icepack.

"Nope. One minute Lou and I were grappling, then he mumbled something I didn't understand. That's when the lights went out." He moaned. "My head is splittin'. I sure hope Jessup got the take, 'cause I don't think I'm up to another fight scene. Not today, anyway."

Ella rushed over and handed me a torn piece of red-checkered plastic that she'd fashioned into an icepack. "Kellyanne isn't at the table. I hope she doesn't get upset that I destroyed her tablecloth."

I thanked her and placed the makeshift cold pack against the crown of Mac Harris' head. "A couple of paramedics will be here soon. They'll give you something for the headache." I also instructed, "Get someone to drive you to the hospital. I'll let the ER know to check you for a possible concussion."

He groaned his thanks and rested his head on top of his crossed arms.

I glanced around, mentally counting the number of people in the room and comparing that number with the names on the call list. The actors had seated themselves around the tables. Barbara Nettles and Sam Jessup sat in their director chairs. Sam looked irritated, while

Barbara appeared to be in a stupor. Gloria Farnham returned from the refreshment table with a cup of coffee for her boss. I overheard her say, "Anyone seen the refreshment lady? We're almost out of coffee."

Maybe Kellyanne had left before the accident. I made a note on the back of the call sheet to mention her disappearance to Dad. I scribbled other notes, too.

Though I only knew Cody by today's appearance, his non-presence seemed so strange that I felt obligated to pin down his whereabouts.

The actors spoke in low tones, clearly sobered by the incident. Some of them gathered around the refreshment table, helping themselves to various liquid refreshments. Someone expressed concern about being in danger.

I whispered to Ella, "Did you see Cody leave?"

She glanced around the movie set. "No, but he's definitely not here."

"Maybe I should go look for him."

"Tullah, you don't think he—"

"I don't think anything, Ella. I'm just curious to know why he isn't here with the other actors. Surely he heard the gunshot."

"Good point. What should I do while you're off exploring?"

Before I could answer, Sally Davenport rushed to stand with us. Her knuckles were white from her tightly clasped hands. She seemed overwhelmed. "Dr. Holliday, ah, never mind. Maybe it was just my imagination."

Her blue gaze was frighteningly intent. She turned to leave. I reached out to touch her arm. "What do you think might be your imagination?"

She hesitated. "I thought I saw Cody on the catwalk."

"You're sure it was Cody?"

She shook her head. "Maybe. Now I'm not sure. I thought I caught sight of someone dressed like Cody, except I didn't see his face."

"Could it have been Lou? I mean, he *is* Cody's stunt double."

Sally shrugged. "Forget it. I don't want to cause trouble." She tucked several strands of blonde hair behind one ear. "Yeah, you're right. It must have been Lou."

"Still," I said, "do you know if there were any changes to the script that Jessup didn't know about?"

"Huh-uh, absolutely not! Jessup is a tyrant. He's in control of all aspects of the filming. If there are any revisions to a script, he has to approve them before they become final. This is the first time I've worked with him and hopefully the last. He can make you feel inept with a single, imperious glance, and it's rumored that he can make and break careers."

"One more question, Sally."

"O-kay." She drew the word out as if annoyed.

"Was there any animosity between Cody and Lou?"

My question seemed to startle her. "It's not my place to say. Honestly, I haven't been with PEP long enough to know who are frenemies, and who are enemies." She sighed heavily. "If you catch my drift."

She excused herself and joined the group milling around the coffee and pastries, talking in small pockets of forced kinship.

My phone rang. Dad's picture popped up on the

screen. His voice was deep and resonant—like a radio announcer. "The door's locked."

In all the disquiet, I'd forgotten about the door. "Be right there."

Dad appeared in the doorway and scanned the movie set. I had no doubt he was memorizing every face in the room. He, Tiny, and Charlie were an imposing force as they entered. Rita and Bubba followed with a gurney.

I guess I need to explain that Charlie is an auxiliary deputy. In fact, Charlie wears many hats—saloon owner, chief of the volunteer fire department, and when Dad needs an extra pair of trustworthy hands, he calls on Charlie, whom you all know is my godfather.

"Bubba?" I pointed. "That's Mac Harris. He's suffered a nasty blow to the head. It's possible he has a mild concussion. Can you give him something to ease the pain?"

"Sure thing. In fact, if he doesn't mind riding with a dead body, we can transport him to the hospital."

Dad walked to where the corpse lay supine on the air mattress. He stooped and lifted the blanket. He looked up at Tiny and Charlie. "Powder burns. Shot at close range." He semi-rolled the body over. "No exit wound."

Dad is all business when it comes to crime. He doesn't mince words. He stood. "Folks," he said peremptorily, eying the group, letting them know he meant business. "Until we can prove the deceased's death was a freak accident, I'm treating this as a crime scene."

Although it'd taken Dad twelve minutes to arrive, and we'd all had time to adjust to death, Dad's announcement had the effect of an exploding bombshell. Reality hit home—hard. A shocked buzz of conversation hummed around the room. A few reactions were marked.

As mysteriously as she had disappeared, Kellyanne Simpson reappeared. She wore a strange smirk on her face. She turned beet red the moment she spotted me watching her.

Dad lifted his voice and spoke clearly. "Deputies Goodbody and Whitehorse will take you out one by one, to a smaller room in the back of the auditorium. Once you've been fingerprinted and they've taken your statement, you may go home, though we'll talk to all of you again later." He let his gaze filter around the room, settling briefly on each face to let them know not to challenge him. "You may carry on business as usual. However, no one is to leave town until I've cleared you."

His face softened when he looked at me. "I'll need you to help with the fingerprinting. You and Ella can come in later this afternoon and give your statements."

Tiny pointed to Sam Jessup. "You sir, come with me."

Jessup's mouth hung open. He looked from Tiny to Dad to Charlie, as if the three had sprouted horns from the tops of their heads. "This is the most denigrating thing I've ever been subjected to. I want my lawyer." Then his mouth snapped shut.

Dad stared at the director with pointed intensity. "Sir, unless you're guilty of murder and wish to confess, you're not being charged with anything, merely being asked to answer a few questions. Of course, if you have something to hide, then by all means you should definitely call your attorney."

I had to turn away and bite my lip to keep from laughing. Sam Jessup looked embarrassed and displeased.

I leaned in close and whispered to Dad, "Cody West, the main star, left the set. It's against the rules to leave even if you're an A-lister. He hasn't returned." I nodded in Sally Davenport's direction. "She thinks she might have seen him on the catwalk seconds prior to the shooting."

"Good to know. Tiny and Charlie can handle the questioning. Let's you and me go on a little hunting trip."

Ella expelled a soft sigh. "Tullah, I'll catch a ride back with Bubba and Rita. Someone needs to open the clinic for this afternoon's appointments. It's all small animal patients, nothing I can't handle."

I reached into my pocket and tossed her the keys. "Take my truck. I'm sure Dad won't mind giving me a ride once we've finished here. I'll check in with you as soon as I get home. Thanks, Ella, you're a gem."

I watched Ella trot toward the door and disappear outside. She had become more than a valued assistant— she was a good friend.

Chapter Six

"Dad, if you don't mind, I'd like to ask Kellyanne a couple of questions."

"I'll be up there." He pointed to where the alleged crimes had been committed.

I casually strolled over to the long table. Kellyanne was brewing a large urn of coffee. She was petite, with serious brown eyes, and hair to match. She used a pair of tongs to rearrange a platter of cookies. A contrite smile flittered across her face. "Terrible. I can't believe such a horrible thing has happened."

"Yeah, I know." I decided to play the *I'm your friend* card. "Do you make your own pastries? The chocolate chip cookies are especially good."

"Heavens, no!" She laughed. "PEP has an account with United Food Distributors. I do have a healthy budget when it comes to ordering. The Hermanns like to keep their crew and actors happy. I even keep a special brand of water for the persnickety ones like Sam Jessup."

I helped myself to a coconut macaroon. "I thought it was against rules to leave the set once filming had begun."

Kellyanne's cheeks pinked. I nibbled on the cookie, giving her time to formulate an answer. "It's not unusual for me to slip out quietly, especially when either the first or second director calls cut or wrap.

There are times when the actors drink and eat more, like today. I also bring in light lunch items—carrot sticks, cucumber sandwiches, that sort of thing."

"Kellyanne, we both know you weren't taking care of food. You came back empty-handed. It'll be easier for you to tell me your whereabouts instead of telling my dad." She poured a large cup of coffee and took her time emptying in four packs of sugar. I knew she was stalling. "My dad is a smart lawman. He'll know you're hiding something."

"Okay…o-kay! It isn't what you think."

"I don't think anything. Tell me."

The smile dried on her face. "I've always wanted to be an actress. I've flunked every audition. My agent even dropped me. I don't have the money to take acting lessons. That's why I took this job as the refreshment lady. I thought if I could observe, I could learn."

"That still doesn't explain why you left the set."

She shrugged. I inwardly cringed when she swallowed a large gulp of sugar with coffee. "Cody has been coaching me." She reached inside an apron pocket and pulled out a note and handed it to me. "He slipped this to me."

In handwriting that resembled chicken scratch, the note said to meet him inside his motorhome after today's wrap. Kellyanne blushed when she said, "We were going to practice a love scene. I guess I'm a little dense."

She ran her finger around the lip of the cup. "Things went beyond practice." She didn't specify the meaning of *things*. "He said he loved me—that I was his girl. It's taken me a while to figure out that he was using me. I was just another girl to him—someone to

43

keep him satisfied.

"I saw him leave and decided to tell him it was over, that I was onto him and there'd be no more freebies, and that I'm...I'm..." She placed her hands over face. Her shoulders shook with silent sobs.

"What happened?"

"Nothing. He wasn't in his coach." She opened her cellphone for me to see where she'd called him. The time matched with his absence from the set. "He didn't answer." She shrugged again and took another large swallow of coffee. "I came back and slipped as quietly as I could through the back door. I saw you looking at me, and I thought maybe you had put two and two together. I was embarrassed."

"Are you sure you're...?" In the event she'd meant something else, I avoided saying the word *pregnant*.

"I took the home test three times." Sarcasm laced her voice. "Yeah, I'm positive."

I wasn't sure what to say. Should I offer my condolences or congratulations? I decided on neither.

"Here's the thing. When my dad questions you, be honest. He's not the least judgmental. He'll respect that you're an adult." Kellyanne looked dismal. I added, "Do you have any idea where Cody might have gone?"

She heaved a sigh. "It's no secret he has a drinking problem. There are times when he slips out between takes to fortify himself with booze. Because Cody is still a big money draw at the box office, Sam and the other directors turn a blind eye." She shook her head. "Since he's not in his motorhome, I have no idea where he might've gone. Maybe try Dominique Dupont. She and Cody were a pretty hot item once."

Hmm. I wondered if Kellyanne was the Miss Prissy

Pants that Dominique Dupont had alluded to. I asked, "What will you do now?"

Her eyes filled with tears. "I have a little money saved. Enough to get me home."

"Where is home?"

"Minnesota."

"What will you do about the baby?"

"I'm not sure. There's just my grandma. She's really old and all I have. I hope she won't be too disappointed in me."

I thought about my grandmother and how she would walk through fire for me, and how much I loved her. "You have options, Kellyanne. Weigh them all before you make any decisions you might regret." I squeezed her hand. "If your grandma is anything like my grandmother, then she'll welcome you *and* a great-grandbaby with open arms."

She pressed her hands against her still flat abdomen. "I hope you're right, Dr. Holliday."

I offered a last smile and made my way up the stairs.

"Dad?"

"Back here."

I hastened to the end of the faux second floor. The area was dim, and I carefully picked my way. The floor was littered with a mass of cords that reminded me of coiled snakes, while overhead were rigged more cameras than I wanted to count right then.

Dad flashed his penlight around. "I'll come back tonight with a bigger light."

"Jessup's not going to like being shut down."

"Too bad. I've already apprised his bosses that until we prove otherwise, this building is considered a crime scene and off limits to everyone. The Hermann brothers assured me I have their fullest cooperation."

I nodded. "Dad, Cody West is apparently a closet alcoholic. If you had to guess, where would he hide his bottle when he needed to sneak a drink?"

He smiled. "Men's room—inside the toilet bowl."

"Makes sense. No one has seen Cody, and he's still missing."

"Then let's go."

On the way down the stairs and around the faux saloon wall to the hall that led to the public bathrooms, I related my conversation with Kellyanne, including about her pregnancy.

"Poor kid. I hope the best for her."

As we neared the doors that opened to the men's restroom, a sense of nagging expectation washed over me. At the door, I hesitated.

"Punkin?" He glanced at me. I guess my expression worried him.

I blew out a deep breath. "It's nothing terrible. At least, I hope not."

He pushed open the door, and I followed. We'd found Cody West. He was curled in a fetal position on the black-and-white tiled floor, passed out cold and snoring away. His hands were folded under one cheek. He wore jeans and boots, a long-sleeved tan shirt, and a vest. It appeared he had stepped on his white cowboy hat and crushed the crown.

The room reeked of body excrement, vomit, and alcohol. The handsome cowboy hero looked more like a skid row bum. At a glance, Cody's gun belt, with holster, was draped over an open stall door. Dad pulled a plastic bag and a pair of evidence gloves from his back pocket. He fitted the gloves over his hands before lifting the revolver from the holster and sniffing the barrel. "It's recently been fired."

He opened the cylinder, unloaded it, and held up an empty casing. "This isn't a blank. It's a hollow-point .44 caliber. It's designed to deform so that all the energy will be converted to tissue damage and not exit." He dropped the spent shell into the baggie.

"So that's why there was no exit wound. The bullet is still inside the body."

Bile rose in my throat, and I forced down the gag when I knelt to check Cody's pulse. "I don't like the blue tinge to his skin. He may have alcohol poisoning."

He nodded. "Call Bubba to see if he and Rita have left yet. We'll need them to transport Mr. West to the hospital to get him sobered up."

"Something's not right, Dad." I swept my hand toward Cody. "Do you think he could have been sober enough to shoot Lou, bash Mac on the head, and then race to the bathroom without being seen?"

"It's possible he's a functioning alcoholic."

I gave this a quick thought. "Which means he appears physically and mentally healthy but really isn't."

"Yep, which means our Mr. West could have actually pulled the trigger."

"Another question… What was his motive? He's rich, has his pick of women, and lives the good life. You know what I mean?"

"Beats me, Punkin."

I made the call. "I caught Bubba in time. They hadn't left the parking lot yet."

Dad huffed out, "What a waste." He pulled several

more bags from his back pocket and filled them with the belt and holster, and Cody's smashed hat.

Bubba and Rita pushed through the door. Bubba checked Cody's vitals. "His pulse is low, breathing is shallow. Thankfully, he didn't choke to death on his own vomitus."

I stood out of the way while Dad helped Bubba load Cody onto the gurney. "Maybe the Hermann brothers will see to it that he gets into a good treatment program. It appears he has a powerful addiction."

Dad squeezed my shoulder. "You have a good heart, Tullah."

I almost missed Dad's compliment. A thought struck me, and struck hard. "Dad, do you think someone is trying to frame Cody? I mean, aren't all prop guns loaded with blanks?"

"That's what we have to figure out. Right now, we'll need to wait until Mr. West is sober enough for me to question."

Chapter Seven

By the time I arrived home, Ella had already closed the clinic. I had phoned early to let her know I was bringing supper.

I invited Dad to join us for BBQ wings. He declined. Before I closed the door to the 4-Runner, he issued a warning. "Thanks for your help today, Tullah. Just remember, you have your own work to do, and I have mine."

I know it's serious when he gives me one of his looks and calls me by my name. I merely nodded. "Are we still on for Sunday?"

"Tanti would have my hide if I missed our Sunday breakfast. Love you, Punkin."

I slammed the door and watched him drive away. River and Rascal dashed around the house to greet me. River sniffed the aroma from the sacks of food. His tail wagged so fast it reminded me of a metronome. "No chicken bones for you, my boy."

Ella met me under the carport. She relieved me of the food while I unlocked the door. "My mom called. She told me about the hospital's special guest."

"Yeah, how's he doing?"

"Considering that she ordered his stomach pumped to get rid of the excess alcohol, and has him on oxygen and IV, I'd say he'll survive."

We set out the food. It had been hours since

breakfast, with nothing to eat except a few cookies and coffee, but I didn't realize how hungry I was until I nearly sucked the meat right off one of the drummies. I told her about Kellyanne.

Ella licked sauce from her fingers. "Part of me wants to feel sorry for her, but the other part wonders why she was too irresponsible to use protection. I mean, it's the twenty-first century. It's not like we're living in the dark ages."

"I suppose people do crazy things when they think they're in love."

Ella shrugged and refilled her plate. "I'm really disillusioned. I believed Cody was the real deal. A hero. A crusader for justice."

"Just like Kellyanne, you're only human. You can invent any fiction and call it life."

For a while we ate in silence—each lost in our own thoughts. Truthfully, I was trying to figure out how to visit Cody in the hospital without my dad's knowledge. "What about Mac Harris? Did your mom say?"

"Has a mild concussion. She cleansed the gash on his head and sent him home with orders to take it easy for the rest of the week. She said he wasn't happy about that, because Hank Boyd needed his help breaking the palomino."

Breaking... I didn't like that word. It implied breaking the horse's spirit. Breaking always meant harsh and sometimes cruel treatment.

Ella interrupted my thought. "Oh, that reminds me. Mr. Boyd called. He wanted to know if you could come to geld Spitfire in his stall any sooner than the date you set earlier. He called the horse a crazy devil and said it had managed to back one of the handlers into a corner and kicked him. Mr. Boyd really doesn't want to risk trying to load Spitfire in a trailer."

"Sure, we can do that. I'll confirm the time with Boyd in the morning."

****

River and Rascal followed me upstairs to my dark bedroom. I peered out the window. The security light showed the empty yard.

It rained that night. The wind chime suspended from the porch eave and raindrops pelting against the windowpane awakened me.

There are some memories that get stuck between your teeth when you sleep, so that when you open your eyes they fly right out at you. It'd been almost two years since Junior Lampson had attacked me. It had stormed that night, too.

I crept downstairs and rechecked my locks. I listened and heard only rain. River and Rascal padded behind me as I rechecked all the windows. I saw nothing but rain. By the security light next to the clinic, I saw only water gushing out the gutter spout.

Nothing else stirred.

Lightning splintered the sky. It had also rained the night Earl Redfern broke into my house and tried to kill me.

Another flash, followed by rolling thunder.

I didn't want the faces of these fiends to be the last thing I saw before returning to bed, so I rearranged the memories as if they were a deck of cards, and thought about my mother. I saw her laughing as we danced around the living room. I was six years old.

I imagined each memory as a grain of sand inside an oyster. Each grain grows into a pearl as the oyster protects itself from the irritating sand, while the shell protects both the oyster and the beautiful pearl inside.

I padded back to bed.

Chapter Eight

I swam up from a deep sleep to find rain continued to patter lightly against the bedroom windowpane. I remembered that it was Saturday. I slept again.

River whined and licked my hand. He seems to know when I'm having a bad dream. I sat up and swung my legs over the side of the bed, trying to shake away the grogginess.

The mellow aroma of coffee wafted upstairs. I caught myself humming as I climbed into the shower, then dressed in a pair of shorts and a T-shirt, and braided my hair. Unless there was an emergency, I planned to spend the day relaxing.

After loading the washing machine, I settled down with my mystery novel but found myself wondering what it takes to kill a person. I set my book aside and opened my laptop to a fresh page and typed:

PEP Murders

Question: Who would want Cody West dead?

I thought about the conversations Ella and I had overheard outside the motorhome.

Possible Suspects: Nikki Lewiki, aka Dominique Dupont, said she'd often thought of different ways to kill Cody.

Lou Cantrell resented Cody getting the accolades while he often risked his life, but Lou is dead. Who killed him?

Kellyanne Simpson, single, almost penniless, pregnant, and claims Cody is the father.

What does it take to kill a person and do it without remorse?

I thought about that question.

Dad had once said that almost anyone could commit murder under the right circumstances. I suppose I could if it came to protecting those I loved or if I was cornered. I had certainly fought for my life on two different occasions. Yet I have to believe that it takes a warped mind to sit back and deliberately plan the death of another person.

Killing another person isn't play-acting, where the director calls, "Cut," and the actor gets two thumbs up and then strolls over to the refreshment table for a cup of coffee.

Speaking of coffee, I returned to the kitchen and poured myself a second cup. I sighed when the landline rang. It seemed I rarely got to enjoy a complete weekend.

"Dr. Holliday, how may I help you?"

"Tullah, it's Sunny Sanders."

"Ella isn't here."

Dr. Sanders chuckled. "I know. I just spoke to her. I have a request."

"Sure, as long as it doesn't include slopping around in mud and manure."

She laughed again. "Scout's honor. I'm performing the autopsy on the stuntman this afternoon. Since you're more schooled in forensics than I am, I wondered if you'd like to assist."

Hot dog and six ways to Sunday. Talk about gifts from nowhere. Now I had a legitimate reason for being at the hospital, and while I was there, who could blame me if I accidently on purpose wandered into Cody's room?

"Yes," I blurted, without thought.

While waiting for it to be time to dress and leave, I couldn't settle on one cleaning chore. I did a little laundry, did a little reading, and made myself a snack.

****

I had braided my hair, changed into a pair of jeans, a striped shirt, and my dress boots, like a comforting uniform. It was all I could do to tamp down the excitement as I drove to the hospital. Part of me missed doing autopsies, though on occasion I do have to perform necropsies. The second reason for my delight—I had a good excuse to visit Cody West.

The first thing I spotted at the hospital was the pair of large white paneled vans with satellite dishes on the top. Logos indicated the trucks belonged to news crews from Lexington and Louisville. While driving around the parking lot I noticed that a majority of the car tags were from out of county. It took more than a few minutes to find a vacant space.

A bevy of reporters and cameramen hovered outside the hospital's entrance. I felt an instinctive urge to hide and then reminded myself that it wasn't me the reporters were after. I was just an anonymous visitor. I blew my breath out and strolled toward the group, although I did my best to skirt around the reporters. One of them called out, "Hey, aren't you Doc Holliday?"

I swore under my breath that if he made one snide remark about being his huckleberry or being related to John Henry "Doc" Holliday, he would taste the business end of my fist. I'm proud of my ancestry, but snide remarks do get tiresome.

Since Enigma no longer has a newspaper office, I don't subscribe to any of the out-of-town papers, nor do I ever purchase a sensational gossip rag from the grocery store. It never occurred to me that someone from the movie set had snapped a picture of me leaning over Lou Cantrell's dead body, and had also given my name.

The reporter said something as he shoved a folded newspaper, photograph prominent, under my nose. I don't recall his words, because I was so appalled at seeing the picture of me and the stuntman that I missed the comment…or was it a question?

I'd once seen a flock of flamingoes at a zoo. It was as if the entire group of pink birds were of one mind and moved in perfect harmony. The reporters reminded me of the flamingoes, all dancing in step with their microphones and cameras shoved toward me. I had no desire to be one of their targets. I might think it's my duty to give an accurate statement to my dad and his deputy, but I didn't have to talk to these people. I felt surrounded. And I was.

I could tell the cameras were running. Questions flew at me from all directions.

"Was Mr. Cantrell's death an accident?"

"Do you think the stuntman was murdered?"

"Why were you on the movie set?"

Before the electronic doors slid open, I answered all of the questions with, "No comment…no comment…no comment."

One of the newsmen stepped in front of me. He reminded me of a hyena smiling merrily before he attacked with a barrage of questions. I wanted him out of my way. I was teetering dangerously on the brink of losing my temper.

Dad rescued me. He loomed up behind the reporters, and motioned me to follow him. I wondered for a moment if they would've held me captive or allowed me to enter the hospital if I hadn't been with the sheriff. He wrapped his arm around me and escorted me through the open electronic doors.

The reporters tried to crowd inside. Dad held up his hand to signal they should back off. I knew the cameras were still running. I swiveled to face the camera, my voice ominous. "This is a hospital. Unless you are sick or in the need of surgery, or if you are an immediate relative of one of the patients, and can prove it, your presence is not warranted."

One of the reporters yelled, "We heard Cody West was here. When can we interview him?"

I offered my best smirk. "I have no knowledge of Mr. West's whereabouts. However, I'm here to perform an autopsy. You know, slice open a cadaver, plunge my hands inside, and lift out the guts. There'll be odious body gases, and sometimes I miss and nick the large intestine and bile tends to spew in every direction landing where or on whom it may. Now, if you can get clearance from the hospital's chief of staff, I'll be happy to have you observe."

I recited this as if it was a magic charm, and it seemed to work. I was certain a couple of the reporters had turned a bit green around the gills. One of them said, "Guess there's no story here."

And just like a flock of flamingos moving in perfect cadence, the reporters followed one another to the parking lot and climbed into their vehicles. I was incredibly pleased with myself. Dad graced me with one of his proud-daddy smiles.

He appeared tired. The lines on his face looked deeper, making him seem at least ten years older. "Have you had any sleep, and what about food?"

"No," he admitted. "Not since five this morning. Are you really here to do an autopsy? I thought I made it clear—"

That's when Sunny Sanders walked up. "I asked Tullah to help me with the postmortem. Even though I'm the medical examiner, I'm not ashamed to admit when I need help."

She glanced at her watch. "Tullah, take the elevator to the basement, room three. Go ahead and suit up. I'll meet you there as soon as I've made sure your dad has food in him."

I smiled as I strolled to the elevator. Dr. Sunny Sanders was scolding my dad for not taking better care of himself, and for once he wasn't arguing back. Could this be the beginning of a beautiful friendship?

I took a detour to the nurses' station.

"Hey, Tullah, have you heard about our secret guest?" Brenda Banner's voice held a conspiratorial tone.

I leaned forward and whispered, "You wouldn't happen to know his room number?"

She waggled her thick brown eyebrows. "He's registered as John Smith. Room thirteen."

"Room thirteen? John Smith—really, Brenda." Everyone knew there was no such room number in the hospital.

She shrugged and grinned. "Not my idea." She

scribbled on a sticky note and handed it to me. One word—paparazzi. Then she nodded toward two men wearing sunglasses and dressed in slacks and golf shirts casually browsing through the small gift shop.

My voice was brisk. "Jerks. There're always a few rogues in the bunch." I gave her an appreciative nod and casually strolled to the elevators and pushed the button for the basement.

Once inside the morgue, I pulled a surgical gown over my clothes, donned a lab coat, and pulled disposable booties over my boots. Dr. Sanders joined me and also suited up. We pulled on gloves and covered our faces with shields. She introduced me to a first-year rotation doctor who was acting as the diener.

After several hours of recording every detail and then extracting the bullet that had pierced the heart before lodging between two spinal discs, Sunny closed the cadaver. She said, "I hope this helps Henry solve the case. I know nothing about bullets." She removed her gloves and tossed them in the hazardous material bin. "I could use a cup of coffee. What about you?"

We removed our lab clothes and left the icebox of a room. "Sunny, did you find anything unusual on Lou's clothing?"

"Like I said, I'm really not schooled in forensics, and the hospital isn't equipped for in-depth forensics. If it helps, I have his clothes stored in a plastic bag."

I assured her that would be quite helpful. "I'll ask Dad if he'd like to watch while I go over each piece of clothing. Okay if I use the morgue?"

"It's at your disposal."

"Great. I'll arrange the time with Dad and let you know."

While we waited for the elevator, I said, "Brenda indicated there are two paparazzi in the waiting area. How can I see Cody without giving away his room number?"

The doors opened, and we stepped inside. "Follow me."

We rode the elevator to the surgical floor and stepped out. "We actually have him stashed in one of the operating rooms." Sunny smiled. "Genius, right?"

I grinned and nodded. "Is he a good patient, or does he expect the royal treatment?"

"He's actually too sick to care. Cirrhosis of the liver."

I tsked. "Does he know about Lou?"

"Henry told him. He also wanted to question Mr. West."

"How'd that go?"

"Mr. West kept saying he couldn't remember what happened after he left the set."

"How'd he react to Lou Cantrell's death?"

She sighed as we approached a small room. "He didn't seem all that upset when Henry told him about the stuntman."

"And the fact that he has cirrhosis?"

"He's an odd man, almost devoid of emotions."

"That or he's a very good actor."

We stood at the door. "I have to make rounds. Catch you later, Tullah."

****

He uttered a sound like a growl. "Who the hell are you?"

"Dr. Tullah Holliday." I walked to his bedside and lifted his chart.

He eyed me. "You don't look like a doctor."

"Actually, I'm a doctor of veterinary medicine."

He laughed until he was overtaken by a siege of coughing. I poured a cup of water and lifted his head. "Take a slow sip and let it trickle down your throat."

He obeyed, lay back, and closed his eyes. His chest heaved as if he had difficulty sucking in a deep cleansing breath. "Unless you've got a bottle of hooch tucked away in your back pocket, why are you here?"

"Hank Boyd wants Spitfire gelded. Since he's technically your horse, do you approve?"

Cody lifted his head and squinted at me. "*Technically*, all the animals belong to PEP. Besides, I have an aversion to large animals, especially horses."

I pulled a chair close to the bed and sat down. "Did you have a bad experience with a horse?"

He scrutinized me with a flinty squint. "If you were a psychiatrist, I might think you're here to analyze me, but a horse doc? Come on, give me a break. Why're you really here?"

Cody West had come close to dying. In fact, he was dying, but he was nobody's fool. He'd pegged me. "My dad is the sheriff. I believe he was here earlier?"

"Yeah, so?"

I agreed with Dr. Sanders—either Cody was void of emotions or a very good actor. I sat back and crossed my legs. He lay with his eyes closed. Red spider-like veins marred his face. He had bruises on each arm. Without all the theatrical makeup, Cody West was far from a handsome matinee idol. Between the facelift, eyelid tucks, and Botoxed lips, he looked almost clownish.

"Tell me about Cody West." I thought if I could get

him to relax he might open up about Cantrell.

He opened one eye. "You tell me."

I cleared me throat. "Cody West, born 1969, which makes you fifty-two; stage age—thirty-eight. German-American, born in Milwaukee, high school jock, college dropout."

A dark flush covered his cheekbones. He listened with a slight smile. "How'd you find out about my age and place of birth?"

"That's what happens when you're a famous movie star. Your private business belongs to the public."

He shivered. "Damned cold in here."

I walked to a cabinet, grabbed an extra blanket and placed it over him. "Better?"

He breathed deeply as if fighting with himself. His voice was quiet. "What the hell. You want to know about me. Here goes—the five stages of Cody West." With each stage he held up a finger. "Stage one: Stanley Eisenbarth, a dyslexic minnow in a world of talented sharks; waiting to be discovered; part-time bartender, part-time dog walker, part-time telemarketer. Stage two: Eisenbarth dies, Cody West is born. Stage three: Money, fancy cars, expensive clothes, beautiful women, and the ever-flowing fountain of booze. Stage four: No Oscar, no Emmy, Oaters out, sci-fi in. Stage five..." He blinked as if trying to clear the moisture from his eyes.

I tried to read the expression on his face—anguish, indifference. He stared at me as if returning from a precipice of memory. He held up his thumb, revealing all five fingers. "Stage five: a washed-up failure, a liar, a cheat, a sinner waiting to visit Hell."

A tumult of emotions filled me when I looked into

Cody's eyes. I could almost feel his soul slipping away.

He rolled to his side, so his voice muffled against the pillow as he declared, "Get out of here. Let me be."

I walked to the door. Before I could call it back, the words flew right out of my mouth. "Kellyanne is pregnant."

Cody rolled to a sitting position. His face was flushed. "I'm sorry. I'm sorry for a lot of things. I'm sorry I took advantage of a starry-eyed, non-talented, young woman who believed me when I said I loved her." He huffed. "It was a lie. My entire life is one colossal lie."

He scrubbed both hands over his face. "The truth is Lou and I had our differences. He was jealous of me and made a few threats. I'm sorry Lou is dead. I'm sorry I can't remember anything beyond leaving the set when Sam called, 'Cut.' Maybe I did kill him—maybe I didn't.

"And here's another truth. I had a vasectomy years ago. Now who's the liar?" He sank heavily into the pillow. "I'm tired. Get the hell out and leave me alone."

An honest confession can slice the hardest heart in two. Cody West had given an award-winning performance, except this time it had come from the heart. Dying is a terrifying prospect. He was a dying man and had no reason to lie.

I stood with my hand on the door handle. "Who hates you enough to frame you for murder?"

Cody's expression bent into a sardonic sneer. "There's too many to name." His throat worked as he swallowed. "And some of them are no farther than arm's length."

A nurse walked in with a tray of food. I excused

myself. I needed to be alone to sort through what I was thinking and feeling.

Chapter Nine

Dr. Paul Ritter looked at me across the table at Grandmother's small apartment. I couldn't tell if he was sniffing the air for a hint of the impending storm or soaking up the aroma of hot-out-of-the-oven banana pecan muffins.

Grandmother's laptop sat open. I peeked at the *Enigma Bulletin*'s headlines splashed across the screen in bold black letters—Storm!

Local forecasters were predicting up to two inches of rain. I turned my gaze to the old doctor. "The weather channel is predicting three inches. It's hard to know who to believe."

"Nope, we're looking at more like six inches, maybe even ten. It's the dog days of August, and Mother Nature makes her swing every ten years." He tapped the side of his nose. "I can tell. It's all in the nose."

Patty looked less than convinced. "How's that exactly, Paul?"

Dr. Ritter touched his nose again. "I can smell it in the air."

I turned my gaze out Grandmother's window. It had become a habit of mine since my mother's death. There's something uniquely serene about being somewhere safe when a storm begins to mount, about being home while the world beyond struggles in the elements. Of course, home for me was back at the two-story house I was born in, grew up in, and still live in with my pets.

I surveyed the still-charred remains of the community building and the partially rebuilt government building. Construction problems and other challenges had repeatedly delayed completion of the much-needed offices.

Many of Enigma's roads remained unpaved. Storms of any magnitude tended to flood the lower-lying areas, which put a strain on the town's emergency equipment and personnel. The two main roads that ran out of and into and around our town were the responsibility of the State, fortunately. And, in my mind anyway, the growing traffic from the robust influx of tourists and the personnel from the movie production company, accompanied by the ominous weather forecast, filled me with a foreboding.

"Why stare out the window, Tullah?" Dr. Ritter interrupted my musing. "I predict the rain isn't going to start until later in the afternoon."

"I believe you," I replied as I watched Dad sprint across the street, his head bent against the wind. I opened the door to let him in. "You're frowning. What's up?"

He removed his hat and set it on the back of the couch. "It's been forty-eight hours and no concrete proof that West killed Cantrell. Dr. Sanders released him from the hospital. A limo picked him up about half an hour ago."

"Are you afraid he'll skip town?"

Dad accepted the cup of coffee Grandmother handed him. He settled at the small dining table. "I have the Hermann brothers' assurance that none of the actors and crew will leave until all have been cleared of suspicion. However, I assured them they can carry on with their film-making."

"Well, there's one good thing about a storm, Henry." Grandmother turned to look at me.

"No crime?" Dad said.

"Murders, specifically. Everyone will be settled in out of the storm."

"I wouldn't be too sure of that," I groused. "Remember Earl Redfern and Junior Lampson?"

Grandmother's eyes rounded, and her mouth formed a perfect O. "Let's change the subject. Henry, has Floyd Alderman, the fire marshal, turned in his report yet? It's been almost three weeks."

"As a matter of fact, Floyd said he'd email his final conclusions tonight. I'll let you know the results."

"Good. I should recommend to the council that his raise be as late as his investigative report." Grandmother swept her hand across the table, inviting us to fill our plates with fluffy scrambled eggs, crispy baked bacon, and yummy muffins.

Patty settled at the table. "Tullah, has Tanti shown you the plans for the new government building? I can hardly wait to move in."

Grandmother reached for the butter. "Don't hold your breath, Patty. The contractors are moving slow as snails. It may be next year before it's finished."

"What about new air-conditioned offices for Dad and Joyce, and a new jail?" I buttered a muffin.

Patty busied herself refilling coffee cups. "As a matter of fact, and thanks to a grant from the State, Tanti wielded her mayoral wand and used her persuasive powers to convince the council that an antiquated jail and law offices did not bode well for our wonderful town."

I lifted my eyebrows in surprise. This was news to me. "Dad, did you know about this?"

"Until now, I didn't know it was official." He leaned down and kissed my Grandmother on the cheek. "Joyce and Tiny will be thrilled."

Grandmother smiled up at him. "I'm sorry we still can't do anything about hiring an extra deputy. You know—budget."

Grandmother's apartment is small. Her dining table comfortably seats three. Dad claimed the rocker, and I sat on the sofa. "Did your search of the upstairs saloon set turn up any evidence?"

While I waited for his answer my mind jerked back to the conversation I'd had with Cody at the hospital.

Who hates you enough to frame you for murder?

Too many to name.

Dad's voice finally regained my ear. "...blood. Sunny said you were going to use the lab to see if you could turn up any clues on Cantrell's clothes. Maybe you can do the same with the blood samples I collected."

I rose and walked to the window. The clouds reminded me of huge wads of gray cotton. The sky was slowly fading from deep blue to dark black. A storm was building, all right. It was building inside of me, and I didn't know why.

It seemed like the words echoed inside my head when I spoke. "The hospital lab isn't equipped for proper forensics. I've contacted Vaneeta to let her know I'm sending the clothes via overnight express. I can include the blood samples."

Dr. Vaneeta Sunreet is a friend from medical school and heads the forensics department at the University of Lexington. She's always willing to help out when I need her expertise.

"Vaneeta said she'd expedite the evidence collection from the victim's clothing and other articles."

I spent the next few minutes detailing my conversation with Cody, and I enlightened Dad regarding the conversations Ella and I had overheard. "Niki Lewiki obviously hated Cody and confessed to Cantrell that she'd often thought of different ways to kill him. But that angle doesn't jibe. I mean, she's an actress, so she's seen Cody and Lou dressed alike hundreds of times. How could she mistake one man for the other?"

Dad said, "At this juncture, I'm ruling her out. The day I interviewed her, she was genuinely upset over Cantrell's death. Plus she has an alibi for the time of the murder."

"Dad, she's an actress."

"Point taken."

Dad scratched through his thick brown hair. "Dr. Ritter, if West was able to walk to the men's room to fortify himself with a couple of swallows of bourbon, could he also be cognitive enough to climb up to the catwalk, shoot the stuntman, then rush back to the bathroom to crawl inside the bottle until he passed out?"

Dr. Ritter mimicked Dad and scratched through his thinning white hair. "I'd say so. Mr. West has apparently built up a certain level of tolerance that allows him to adequately function. However, with his recent collapse, I'd say his liver's ability to operate is rapidly declining."

Dad huffed a sigh. "So that still leaves him as my prime suspect."

I swallowed the forkful of eggs I'd put into my mouth. "Did Sunny give you the bullet we retrieved from Cantrell?"

He nodded. "Yep, and it was definitely fired from West's gun."

"What about fingerprints on the gun?"

"Inconclusive. Tiny dusted. Either the prints were wiped clean or the shooter wore gloves."

Dad pushed back his chair and rose and stretched. "What's on your schedule, Punkin?"

"If you mean today—home, reading my mystery novel, and listening to the rain, unless an emergency crops up. I'm scheduled to geld the new stallion Hank Boyd purchased to replace the aging stunt horse. If it's storming tomorrow, I'll call and reschedule for Tuesday."

"That's my girl. Thunder, lightning, and a dangerous horse is chancy, even if he is tranquilized."

I thought for a minute. "It just occurred to me—according to Cody, in this day and age, western movies don't do well at the box office. If that's true, then why would Boyd spend needless money on a horse, especially one that's unbroken and dangerous? Not only that, this came straight from Cody's mouth—he doesn't like animals, especially horses."

"If you ask me"—Grandmother was packing up a couple of muffins for Dr. Ritter—"nothing in the movie business makes sense. Maybe it's a tax write-off." She waggled her shoulders. "Whatever the reason, I just hope PEP keeps the money rolling in. I've even hoped they would extend their contract and make more movies here in Enigma."

Patty chimed in. "Yes, four million dollars goes a long way in our little community."

"What will you do if PEP and the tourists leave and the money dries up?"

"Tullah, stop being a pessimist. Tanti and I might be old, but our brains are firing on all cylinders. We have a cache of ideas that will continue bringing in seasonal visitors."

I merely smiled and returned my gaze to the window. Truth be told, I was in a hurry to return home. I needed to check on my horses and a few recuperating patients.

With the storm drawing closer, Grandmother gave me the perfect out. "I don't mean to hurry you off, Tullah, but I'll feel better knowing you're not driving in a torrential downpour."

Dad forced a sigh. "I've got to go too. I don't know what it is about rain that makes people drive like idiots. I'm afraid Tiny and I are in for a long wet night." He fastened his sheriff's hat in place.

I said my goodbyes, pulled on my rain jacket, and headed out to my truck.

Chapter Ten

Death is not the greatest loss in life. The greatest loss is what dies inside us while we live.

Norman Cousins was a world peace advocate. I recalled his words and thought how poignant they were, especially now that I'm dying.

She had called me in the middle of the night. I didn't want to answer the phone. I was exhausted from my stay in the hospital. I wanted a drink...needed a drink. Someone had come to my motor coach and filched my supply of bourbon. My skin itched, my head ached, and I needed to anesthetize myself against the demons of my past.

Damn her. Damn Tullah Holliday for stirring up memories best forgotten. What right did she have to check into my past?

I silenced the phone and was slipping back into blissful oblivion when the buzzing started again. Maybe it was Joel or Barry. Maybe they were rescinding my contract. Who could blame them? This wasn't the first time they'd paid for me to go into rehab.

My stomach cramped and my hands trembled. I answered, "What!"

"*There* you are." Her voice sounded husky and damned sexy.

I tried to control my jitters. "You're surprised I didn't answer right away. *It's two o'clock in the morning."*

"I'm sorry, darling."

I regretted my sarcasm when she didn't bite back at me with a smart-ass comment. I rolled to the side of bed and stared out into the rain-shrouded night.

"Cody, darling, are you in pain?"

"Damn right. My gut is on fire, and it feels like I have snakes slithering around inside my head."

"Meet me in ten minutes at the barn."

"Are you crazy? It's storming."

She cooed. "I have your favorite. You know, the one with that little hint of brown sugar. If you want it badly enough, you'll come to me."

"I don't want—"

"You know you do, Cody. I have three bottles, and I can get more. You know I can."

I dropped my head into my free hand. I wanted to be strong-willed.

"I talked to the doctor. The prognosis is so sad, my darling. But you know what they say?"

"Enlighten me. What do *they* say?"

She purred. "When life gives you lemons, then drink more bourbon, of course."

"Yeah. Sure. I just…I'm trying to come to terms with it."

"It's a lot to deal with. Don't live…don't live in misery, Cody."

"I'm a screw-up. I've always been a screw-up."

"I have the perfect medicine. All you have to do is meet me in the barn. I love you," she responded and hung up the phone.

She loved me, all right. In her own twisted way. That was the part that always messed with my head. A memory flashed in my mind's eye. We'd had one of our memorable fights. She'd choked me. I'd spit in her face, and then she'd really let me have it.

Cramps nearly doubled me over. A bout of dry heaves left me gasping. She had in her possession the only medicine I needed. An overwhelming longing sprang up inside me.

Although the rain was still falling heavily, soaking my hair, jacket, and jeans, I somehow trudged through the mud. Part of the time it seemed like I was leaning on someone, being helped along. It didn't matter. The thought of smooth amber liquid burning its way down my throat and into my stomach drove me faster until I reached the barn.

The smell hit me. Manure and horse piss mingled with wet hay. I bent to grasp my knees and retched. Starlight reached his head over the gate and nickered. The horse hated me as much as I feared him. They say animals have a sixth sense about such things. I walked to the far side of the aisle to avoid getting nipped.

"Stanley...over here." Her voice was smooth as silk.

Stanley? No one ever calls me that anymore. No one except...

"Where?"

"I'm here."

Lightning flashed. She looked straight at me, a smile on her face. She was dark-haired, young, and slender. Her jeans fit like a second skin. She held up both hands. A meager light in the barn glinted off the two bottles of my favorite. She lifted a bottle to her mouth and pulled hard. A little liquid escaped and dribbled from the corner of her mouth. I wanted to rush over and lap it up.

She held it forward and laughed wildly, her head thrown back. "Stanley, oh, Stanley, you vain and silly man, don't you know when you're being played?"

She jogged to the open end of the barn and out into the rain. The bourbon beckoned, the snakes in my head rattled, and hot coals scalded my guts. "Come back! Don't go." I trotted after her.

I grabbed her arm and spun her around. She allowed me to snatch the bottle from her hand, and laughed as I nearly choked while sucking down that precious amber salvation. So enraptured with the liquid pleasure, I barely felt the needle when it pierced the skin and sank between my ribs in an upward motion. I know nothing about anatomy, but in that one stupid moment, I knew she had punctured my heart.

I clutched the bottle to my chest as I wilted into a muddy puddle.

She smiled down at me with her fanatical blue eyes.

I heard each beat of my heart.

Horses. Starlight. Spitfire.

Thud.

I writhed where I fell.

Thud.

Powerful hooves pounded my chest.

Thud.

Someone screamed. Maybe it was me.

Thud.

I could see the porcelain gleam of her teeth as she smiled that terrible smile.

It's true what they say. Your past does flash before your eyes before you die.

It was too late…too late to relive my life.
I waited for the next thud.
If it came, I never knew it. Not in this world.

Chapter Eleven

Water splattered my face. I struggled in waist-deep mud. Horses were screaming. I was screaming. I swam up from the dream as River whined and licked my hand. I squinted at the clock. Four thirty.

River climbed on the bed to lie next to me. He laid his head on my chest and whimpered. I assured him that I was okay. Except I wasn't. The dream lingered, leaving me disoriented as I stumbled to the bathroom to splash cold water over my face.

Urgency filled me. Charlie and Grandmother had often said there are different types of dreams and we should heed them, especially the warning dreams that presage feelings of threat or menace, and dread, and even death, in a particular way.

I pulled on a pair of jeans and a blue T-shirt. The skies had opened up and dumped several inches of water over the yard. Unless a heifer was birthing triplets or a sow needed a cesarean section (I'm joking, of course), I didn't expect to be bombarded with clients.

I padded downstairs to the kitchen and peered out the window. It certainly wasn't weather for enjoying coffee on the front porch. At first, I saw nothing except rain and a dim light from Ella's trailer.

I opened the back door and inhaled the clean, washed air. My heart sped up. *Is this a trick?* I grabbed an umbrella and walked down the steps and around my truck. River and Rascal followed. At first it appeared that someone, playing a cruel joke, had dumped a load of black boulders between my house and the clinic. I stepped forward for a closer look.

River bounded toward the huge rocks. His deep barks issued a volley of warnings. Chuffing a series of high-pitched brays, Rascal trotted after his buddy.

The outside security light revealed six vultures. They turned their ugly, wrinkled, red heads to stare at me. One vulture spread its enormous black wings, the others did the same, and like a wave, one after the other, the first one lifted off the ground and the others followed suit, all of one vulture mind. Wings lifted as the Labrador and donkey plunged forward. I watched as the ominous black carrion eaters flapped toward the 4-H fairgrounds.

Cousin Uma swears that vultures are pallbearers in the sky. She says that when we see them circling over a certain area they are waiting for something to die or have found something that's already dead.

I squeezed my eyes shut and silenced my clamorous mind for a second. An inner voice spoke. *Spitfire.*

What did it mean? I hated these puzzles that winged their way to me as if I were a genius who could instantly put all the pieces together.

I waited for my pulse to calm. In my mind's eye, I saw a horse rearing, and screaming filled my ears. There was blood and a man's blank face. I held all of this in my mind's eye until the picture broke away into disjointed blue and black shapes. I was seeing my dream in real time.

The air was thick with heat. My only goal was to

get to the fairgrounds as quickly as possible. The skies opened up again. I raced to Ella's trailer and pounded on the door and called her name.

She yawned. "It's barely four thirty. What's the emergency?"

"We're about to find out. Help me hitch up the horse trailer."

She opened the door and peered out. "Tullah, you're scaring me."

"I'm scaring myself."

We slogged through the mud, our clothes soaked to our skin. Looking up at the sky was like looking into a dark abyss. And this, the forecasters had warned, was just the beginning. Thankfully, the rain had slowed to a drizzle as we set out down my long driveway and turned toward the road that led through town and onward to the fairgrounds.

The sign *Welcome To Enigma* appeared in a distant view. I turned off at a newly painted sign that announced *Premier Entertainment Productions. No unauthorized vehicles beyond this point.*

A sudden deluge of rain peppered the windshield. Wind caused the horse trailer to sway sideways as I rounded the final bend in the road and encountered the tall gate and the fence that encircled the 4-H livestock area. I gripped the steering wheel and eased on the brake. We had skirted around motor home city. All appeared quiet.

I slowed to a stop. Ella jumped out. "I'll get the gate."

Through the rhythmic slash of windshield wipers, nothing moved. In fact, the entire area looked deserted. Ella waved me through. I waited for her to hop in the truck. My assistant had remained quiet during the drive. After a year of working with me, she seemed to have gotten used to my quirks. Flinging wet hair out of her face, she said, "Tullah, is this one of those times when you're having one of your—weird episodes?"

"I had a dream. Call me crazy, but I think Spitfire is in danger." I didn't tell her about the man in my nightmare.

"Who would want to harm that beautiful palomino? I'm sure with time and the proper training he'll make a wonderful stunt horse."

"Your guess is as good as mine." I swung the truck around, put it in reverse, and backed the trailer up to the barn's wide entrance. "In a storm like this, the barn's sliding double Dutch doors should be closed."

"Yeah, I noticed. Both the front and rear are wide open."

I shifted into reverse and backed the trailer down the wide aisle several feet inside the dark building. If I had to load horses, especially a wild one, I wanted to make sure my trailer blocked the outside entrance to keep the horse from escaping.

Once inside, I walked to a wall and flipped a switch. Light flooded the darkened interior. On both sides of the aisle, several horses stuck their heads out of their stalls. Urgency filled me. Two stall doors at the end of the wide aisle stood open. Starlight and Spitfire's stalls were empty.

"What idiot would leave two valuable horses outside in this kind of weather? C'mon." I picked up my pace. "Look," I pointed. The sliding rear Dutch doors that led to the outside corrals gapped wide.

A man's voice yelled, "Hey, who the hell's in

here? This is private property."

I glanced over my shoulder. Technically it wasn't private property, but that was a moot point.

A ruffled Hank Boyd with his shirt half tucked inside the waist of his jeans trotted down the aisle. It wasn't his disheveled appearance that concerned me but rather the rifle he carried.

"It's me, Dr. Holliday."

He seemed confused. "It's Monday. I thought you weren't coming until tomorrow to get Spitfire."

I noticed he kept a tight grip on the rifle.

"I thought the storm might've upset him. I've come to check on him."

By this time Hank had reached us. I pointed. "The stalls are empty."

Hank scratched his scruffy chin. "Can't trust anyone. I don't know how many times I've told the barn help to double-check the stall latches before turning in for the night. Someone's gonna catch hell when I find out who didn't."

I climbed over the corral's wooden rails. Spitfire appeared like an apparition out of nowhere. He stood on hind legs, his forelegs pawing at me. His eyes were crazy wild, and his lips were drawn back over large yellowed teeth. He landed on all fours and lunged. I stepped backward.

Hank Boyd yelled, "Step aside so I can get a clean shot."

"No." I flung my arms wide situating myself between Boyd and the horse. "He's frightened. I can calm him."

"He's a killer. Should've already euthanized him, but *no,* the brothers say he has potential. *Potential*, my ass. The potential to kill or seriously maim someone."

Ella shouted, "Listen to Tullah. She has a special way with animals."

Out of the corner of my eye, I saw her swing a leg over the top rail. "Don't, Ella. Stay where you are."

"Okay."

"Hank, trust me. I need you to get out of the corral. Please, let me handle this."

"Have it your way, but if he knocks you down, he's a dead horse."

"Fair enough." In my heart of hearts I knew my mother's spirit was watching over me. A loud clap of thunder spooked Spitfire. He reared and pawed the air and tossed his magnificent golden head. I placed my hands forward, palms up, and crooned the words of the ancient Cherokee.

In the shadows stood Starlight, his head down, mud clinging to his body. I feared the old horse, having stood in the pouring rain all night, might contract pneumonia. I continued to croon. About the time I had Spitfire where I could grab hold of his halter, lightning streaked across the sky. The bright flash frightened the palomino and sent him racing across the paddock.

It was that same flash that sent electrifying terror down my spine. The light had illuminated the water trough and, jutting from behind the trough, where Starlight stood, was a pair of muddied boots attached to a pair of muddy, jean-clad legs.

Chapter Twelve

The skies had opened up again. Rain slashed at my face as I eased toward the body for a closer look. Mud sucked at my boots, making it difficult to lift my legs. I lost my footing and landed on one knee.

"Careful, Tullah," Ella warned.

Fighting the rain even for that short distance left me panting. Sludge oozed between my fingers as I struggled to regain my balance. Hank Boyd straddled the top rail, the rifle jacked against his shoulder. He shouted against the rain's thunderous roar. "Who is it?"

Before I could answer, a horse screamed. I turned in time to see Spitfire rear, pawing the air. I looked the stallion in the eyes, the palms of my hands stretched forward. I spoke soothing words.

Thunder vibrated the ground.

Spitfire reared again.

Ella screamed, "No!"

A rifle shot and thunder blended into one massive explosion.

My muscles tensed. Did Hank Boyd have a personal vendetta against the palomino stallion? Fury raged inside me until I spotted the rifle spiraling upward and Boyd's arms flailing like a comedic acrobat. I almost laughed when a tsunami of mud washed over him.

My eyes cut to the stallion. His posture was taut

with readiness. Starlight had raced to the other side of the corral. His sodden body trembled. I shifted my attention to Ella. She wore a grin, and the way she spread her hands wide, I knew she'd deliberately knocked Boyd off the fence. I gave her two thumbs up. She climbed to the ground and grabbed the rifle. "Tullah, are you hurt?"

I cupped my hands around my mouth and yelled, "Thankfully, when you knocked the rifle upward, the bullet went astray."

"Do you think it's"—she nodded toward the trough—"one of the handlers?"

It was as if the mud desired to hold Boyd captive as he tried several times to stand. Once he regained his footing, he trudged toward me.

I squatted over the body. The man's arms were held against his chest. Clutched in his left hand was the neck of a broken bourbon bottle. His eyes looked into mine, but they were motionless. There was no need to check for a pulse. I touched my chin to my chest and whispered his name. Only the corral's sullen silence and the patter of rain on my head and shoulders answered me.

"Damn. It's…" Boyd stood over me and gagged. Once he caught his breath, he commanded, "Give me my rifle. That horse needs killin'."

"Ella," I yelled above the storm. "Call my dad. It's Cody West, and he's dead." I also instructed her to back the horse trailer all the way down to the barn's open outer doors.

My heart pitched with anger. "Mr. Boyd, I'm taking custody of both horses until the cause of Cody's death is determined."

His hands shot out. He grabbed me by both wrists and yanked me up. "Determined? The hell you say. It's obvious that killer stomped Cody to death."

Anger pulsed through me at being manhandled. "Cody was terminally ill. None of us know right now just when exactly he died, or if he died from the disease or was truly stomped to death."

And then Boyd laughed—a loud hysterical cackle. "Spitfire is a rogue. You'll never get him loaded." He shifted his weight and nearly touched my nose with his outstretched finger. "I'm head wrangler for PEP. I'm boss over the animals. What I say goes. He stays here. *¿Comprendes?*"

I fired back. "And I am the medical director for Engima County Animal Control. I am within the law to confiscate any animal that I deem dangerous or in danger. *¿Comprendes?*"

Ella had backed the trailer so that it blocked most of the barn's rear entrance. I instructed her to open the truck doors to seal off any possible escape route. I also instructed Hank Boyd to make himself invisible. "It's obvious Spitfire doesn't trust you. Don't move, and don't make a sound until Starlight and Spitfire are loaded."

"I'll have you fired for this. I'll recommend the Hermanns rescind their contract with the town council. Think of the millions your little Podunk town will lose, and it'll be your fault. Is a horse worth all that money?"

He stood with his arms folded across his chest. Fire glinted in both eyes. I was soaked to the skin, cold, hungry, in desperate need of coffee, and in no mood for a staring match. "Mr. Boyd." I spoke through gritted teeth. "When Sheriff Holliday gets here, you can lodge a complaint with him. In the meantime—stay out of my way."

My emotions were getting quite a workout. Inhaling deeply, I beckoned my inner peace. It had been a long day, and it wasn't even time for the sun to rise. Out in the gloom, the red burning tip of a cigarette indicated that Hank Boyd stood outside the corral. What part of *I wanted him gone* did he not understand?

I shifted my gaze and motioned for Ella to come close. Disgust laced her voice. "I'd like to kick that guy in the nuts."

Her revelation was startling. I was tempted to tell her I'd hold Boyd while she gave him her best shot. Instead I said, "Call my dad and explain the situation with Boyd and Spitfire. Tell him to keep the sirens silent. Another thing, keep an eye out. The last thing we need is people gathering around."

She nodded her agreement. "Are you going to give Spitfire one of your special magic potions?"

"You know it. We need to get him calm. Otherwise, I hate to think of the alternative." I climbed between the railings and trotted toward my truck. I inserted a key and opened the panel where I store pharmaceuticals. An automated light flashed on. I needed to get close enough to entice Spitfire to swallow a double dose of TCH's Magic—a combination of herbal ingredients that included valerian root.

"Tullah, what about Starlight?"

"I'm not worried. He's been trailered enough that I'm confident he won't hesitate to load."

"I hope you're right." She held the cellphone to her ear.

I mentally calculated Spitfire's weight and the

amount of time it would take the four cubes of my magic concoction to take effect. In a perfect world, perhaps ten minutes. Unfortunately we don't live in a perfect world.

The rain had finally stopped. That was the good news. The bad news was a heavy fog had begun to settle over Enigma, turning the familiar night into an eerie landscape. I entered the paddock. Against a fretful moon, Spitfire and Starlight appeared as ghostly apparitions.

I stood perfectly still as the old stunt horse hobbled toward me. His warm breath whispered against my cheek as I gently clutched the halter's cheek strap. I crooned as I rubbed my free hand down his muddied neck. I feared for Starlight's health. He trembled, and not from fear. The rattle in his chest, the runny nose, and persistent cough could only mean one thing—pneumonia.

Ella stood at the gate. "I talked to Uncle Tiny. He said he passed the word on to Bubba and Rita so they'd also come in silent."

I acknowledged the information with a nod. Keeping my voice low and even, I said, "Open the gate and swing it so that it closes off the path between the adjoining corrals. If Spitfire decides to bolt while we're loading Starlight, all possible escape routes will be cut off."

Ella lifted the latch and rushed to secure it as I had instructed. "What else can I do?"

The old gelding walked stiff-legged. Standing for hours in the rain and mud had aggravated his advanced stage of arthritis. "Don't worry, boy, there's a nice warm stall with fresh water, sweet feed, and clover hay waiting for you. As soon as I get you loaded, we'll give you something to ease your pain."

I called to Ella to mix a dose of white willow bark with a scoop of sweet feed for Starlight. She hustled to comply.

It seemed the old horse understood my words. He uttered a series of raspy nickers. Without hesitation he followed me up the ramp and into the trailer. Ella closed and secured the divider gate while I stepped out of the side escape door. We smiled when we heard the horse lipping the feed.

"Will he make it, Tullah?"

I knew what she meant. "We'll do our best to make sure he does." I blew out a steadying breath and patted my pocket. "Let's hope this works."

"Be careful, Tullah."

The weather had taken its toll on Spitfire. The young stallion shivered while keeping a wary eye on me as I slowly approached. My best estimation was that it had been hours since his last meal. I spoke softly, my outstretched hand holding four cubes of tasty morsels. If I'd figured correctly, in about ten minutes he would start feeling the effects of TCH's Magic.

His muscles bunched. He swung his head from side to side, flinging clumps of mud from his mane. He was warning me that I was in his domain and he was the boss.

"Easy, big boy, I'm not your enemy. We're both wet and cold and hungry. I'm as out of sorts as you are." I stopped talking and started singing a Cherokee lullaby my mother used to sing to me when I was frightened.

Hush, little baby, don't be afraid. It's gonna be all

right. I won't let you out of my sight. Hush, little baby, don't be afraid. Oh, my little one, I'll always hold your hand. Dry your tears and weep no more. Hush, little baby, don't be afraid.

With each word I inched forward, my left hand outstretched. Spitfire stretched his long neck. He lipped my hand. All four nuggets disappeared. I dared to stroke the horse's massive cheek and felt the vibration of his jaws as he pulverized the herbal cubes.

I ventured to rub my hand down his neck, his withers, along his back, and all the while crooning the lullaby. He heaved a sigh, and his muscles slowly uncoiled. "Good fella."

I heard the vehicles. So did Spitfire. His ears pricked forward. I felt him tense.

Bad timing.

Ella sprinted around the trailer and truck. I hoped she'd gone to warn whoever had arrived to not slam their car doors shut.

I gave a slight tug on Spitfire's halter. He didn't resist. Mud sucked at his hooves and at my boots, making squishy sounds. The short walk across the corral seemed like a mile. We reached the gate's wide gap. I continued to croon.

Ella peered around the trailer. She mouthed, "It's your dad."

I walked Spitfire to the trailer. I stepped up the ramp. Spitfire balked. I needed to get him loaded before curiosity seekers began to arrive. In a low, even voice, I said to Ella, "Get Dad and Tiny. We'll need to cowboy Spitfire in." Dad and Tiny might be lawmen, but they are also true cowboys and know how to handle stubborn animals.

Tiny said, "You look beat, Tullah."

I was too tired to answer but managed a nod.

Once again, I led Spitfire to the trailer. This time he stepped up the ramp before balking. Dad and Tiny stood on each side of the horse. They interlocked their hands under his tail. Dad said, "Ready?"

On three, Dad and Tiny each placed a broad shoulder against a muddied golden haunch and with one massive push forced Spitfire into the trailer. While Dad secured the stall gate, I tied Spitfire to keep him from rearing.

Once outside, I sat on the running board before my knees buckled. I was in serious need of sustenance.

Chapter Thirteen

Hank Boyd sprang forward. "Sheriff, I demand you arrest this woman." He pointed a finger at me. "I don't give a damn who she is, and if you play the nepotism card, then I have connections that'll make sure you never wear a badge—"

It wasn't my dad who shut down Boyd. It was Tiny. Like my godfather Charlie Whitehorse, Deputy Tiny Goodbody is a gentle giant until someone pushes the wrong button. "Mr. Boyd, I'd advise you to zip your lip unless you'd like me to do it for you. You can either stand over there out of the way, or I can cuff you and escort you to the squad car for threatening an officer of the law. Choice is yours."

Whatever Boyd's next words might have been, they fell away. He pulled another cigarette from his pack and stepped aside.

Dad shot me a look that said to let him take over. I knew he respected my knowledge and ability to handle most situations, but I wasn't law enforcement, and it was time to let him do his job.

He peered at me. "Where's the body?"

I pointed. "Behind the horse trough. It's not a pretty sight, Dad."

This declaration was met with silence.

He motioned for Tiny to join him.

"Dad, I'll need to move my truck so Bubba can get

the ambulance close to the gate. The mud is too deep to roll the gurney inside the pen."

Ella stepped on the running board. "I'll do it, Tullah. I'd rather stay with the horses."

I nodded my appreciation. "Tiny, I hope Ella doesn't ever decide to leave Enigma. She's not only an excellent assistant, but a good friend."

Tiny grinned his appreciation at the compliment I'd paid his niece.

The sun had finally broken through the fog. The temperature had changed from cool to humid. Sweat had begun to pool in my armpits. To avoid contaminating the scene any more than it already was, I'd refrained from covering the body. Part of me wanted to lag back. I had no desire to take a second look at Cody's battered face.

Dad grimaced as he squatted. He took in the entire scene—mud plowed with hoof prints, and water cascading over the edge of the trough like an overfilled waterfall, creating more sludge. Cody clutched the broken bourbon bottle against his chest as if he were protecting it. Tilting his head up to look at me, Dad asked, "Suicide?"

Tiny used his cellphone to snap photos at different angles. You'd think a man Tiny's size and being a lawman would make him immune to grisly sights. I thought he looked a little green around the gills, and who could blame him. The steel horseshoes had virtually destroyed a once-handsome face.

Tiny focused the camera for another shot. "He certainly had reason to take his own life. I mean, being diagnosed with cirrhosis of the liver is like being handed a death sentence."

I slowly let my breath go. "While it seems reasonable, I'm not quite sure I buy the suicide angle."

Dad arched his eyebrows upward. "Why's that, Punkin?"

"I'm not totally disagreeing with either of you. It's just that Cody was afraid of horses. Why would he come inside the corral?"

Dad met my words with silence. I knew he was weighing my question. "You've heard of suicide by cop, where an individual deliberately acts in a threatening manner with the intent of provoking a lethal encounter with law enforcement because they'd rather die than face imprisonment or even the death penalty." He pointed to the broken bottle. "Liquid courage."

"Makes sense, I suppose. Maybe Cody didn't want to suffer, to live in pain knowing there was no cure, so knowing Spitfire was dangerous, he chose the horse as his executioner."

"Exactly. How long do you think he'd been dead before you found him?"

I did a quick calculation. "Ella and I arrived at five o'clock. I remember because I checked the dashboard clock. By the time we found Cody, it was approximately ten after five. His body had already begun to stiffen. As you know it takes one to two hours for rigor mortis to set in, and a full twelve hours for it to vanish. What time is it now?"

Dad glanced at his watch. "Seven thirty."

"Then I'd put his death between midnight and three this morning."

Bubba and Rita arrived, toting the gurney since the muddy ground made it impossible to push the stretcher. Bubba sleeved away the sweat that dotted his forehead.

"Once we load the body, I'll need one of you to help me carry the gurney to the bus. It's too heavy for Rita."

He looked down. "Ready for me to drape a sheet over him, Henry?"

Dad removed a clean handkerchief from his pocket. Since the body had stiffened, he had to pry the fingers loose from the bottle's neck. He dropped the broken piece into the plastic bag that Tiny had supplied. "I'll trust your instinct, Tullah. Tiny'll dust for fingerprints."

To Bubba, Dad said, "He's all yours."

I knew if the only prints found belonged to Cody, then there'd be no question that he'd taken his own life. I figured the paparazzi would have a field day reporting a once-famous movie star's death.

"Tullah, you talked to West last night. Did he mention any next of kin?"

I shook my head. "He didn't, but Kellyanne Simpson, the young woman who runs PEP's refreshment stand, confided in me that she's pregnant and Cody is the father."

Dad pulled at his bottom lip. "Tiny, let's bring Ms. Simpson in. Assure her she's not in any trouble. We're merely seeking information."

I was about to reveal that Cody had denied being the father. That he'd had a vasectomy. I decided to keep that bit of information quiet for now. It didn't matter if Cody had taken his own life or not, there was something fishy about Kellyanne's pregnancy announcement, and I intended to find out what it was.

After his body was loaded, Tiny helped Bubba transport the gurney to the ambulance. Dad and I followed. Suicide? It all seemed so cut and dried. There were no culprits to be tried and prosecuted.

"Do you have a heavy schedule today, Punkin?"

"Not so much. Just routine stuff."

He wrapped an arm around my shoulder. "You look done in."

I enjoyed these rare moments of tenderness. "Nothing that a shower, clean clothes, food, and several cups of coffee can't cure." The thought of food caused my stomach to growl.

"That's my Punkin." He chuckled, then wrinkled his nose. "If you weren't such a mess, I'd buy you breakfast."

We arrived at my truck. "Hey, you're not getting off that easy. It's BBQ night at Charlie's." I waggled my eyebrows at him.

Ella peered out the open window. "Did someone say BBQ?"

Death was no laughing matter, but laughter seemed to ease the distress of what we'd all witnessed today.

I didn't argue. Before rounding to the passenger side, I said, "I'm sorry, Dad."

He cocked an eyebrow. "About what?"

"With Cody dead, you've lost your prime suspect." I shrugged. "The question now is—who killed Lou Cantrell?"

Bubba was pulling out of the barn when a fancy golf cart blocked the ambulance. Two men dressed in designer jeans and snakeskin boots stepped out. Hank Boyd trotted toward them.

Dad said, "That's Joel and Barry Hermann. They're twins."

"Not identical, apparently."

"Nope. The taller one is Joel." Dad coughed. I

supposed he wanted to hide the slight when he said, "The shorter one is Barry."

I glanced from one to the other. Fraternal twins. At least it would be easy to tell the brothers apart. Their shared commonality was their balding heads and pudgy waistlines.

"Boyd must have called them about Cody. I wonder what wild tale he has told them."

"We're about to find out."

Dad's voice was deep and resonant, like that of a radio host. "I was about to notify you. I'd like you to meet my daughter, Dr. Tullah Holliday."

Glancing at my muddied hands, the brothers forewent the handshake. I could see their resemblance to their nephew, Frankie Apollo, being chubby wimps with overly inflated egos and probably bank accounts to match, and hands that had undoubtedly never seen a hard day's labor.

Joel was apparently the spokesman. "Is it true...about Cody?"

Dad nodded. "It is."

"The horses...killed him?"

"It appears that way."

Barry said, "In the movies, it's customary for the next of kin to identify the body. Since Cody had no known family that we're aware of, should my brother or I identify him?"

"Mr. Hermann...Barry...that's not necessary."

"Why not? I mean, in the movies..."

"This isn't a movie script, sir. However, he was your employee." Dad yelled, "Bubba, these gentlemen wish to identify the corpse."

Bubba climbed down from behind the steering

wheel. "Anything you say, Sheriff." He walked to the rear ambulance's doors and swung them wide. He looked at me and winked.

What followed next was like a script out of a comedic drama. Joel Hermann said, "You go first, Brother."

Barry squeaked. "I'm not sure I want to do this. I've never seen a real live dead body."

"Oh, stop your whining," Joel scolded. "How horrible can it be? I mean, we see dead dummies all the time. Think of it as looking at a movie prop without the makeup. Besides, he isn't alive. He's dead."

"Then you go first, Mr. Know-it-all."

Joel made a sound of disgust. He held out his hand. "Oh, come on. We'll do it together. Help me up."

Dad, Bubba, Tiny, and I watched as Joel Hermann lifted the sheet with Barry peering over his shoulder. Joel didn't make a sound. He simply wilted to the floor in a dead faint. Barry jumped to the ground and bent over. Whatever he'd had for breakfast he dumped all over his expensive snakeskin boots.

Chapter Fourteen

We made the drive home in silence while I pondered the circumstances of Cody's death. Part of my brain said to mind my own business. The other part questioned whether or not it was realistic to assume a rich and famous actor had chosen the very thing he feared most to end his life. I didn't realize we had arrived until Ella turned off the ignition. She had parked close to the barn.

A loud rapping on the window snapped me out of my reverie. I looked up to find Grandmother standing next to the door. She held up a large brown sack.

I opened the door and was greeted by a rush of hot air. "I didn't see you following us."

"I did." Ella opened the driver's side door. "You were totally zonked out from seeing—" She shivered. "I don't even want to think about it."

I stepped to the ground, and caught the hint of a smile when Grandmother said, "You look like something the cat dragged in and didn't want. You girls get cleaned up, and I'll put breakfast on the table."

"I take it you've talked to Dad."

Grandmother was a beautiful, intelligent woman. At seventy-plus years old, her face was completely unlined, framed by a mass of black hair threaded with silver, and slicked back into her signature bun at the nape of her neck. "I'm sorry you and Ella had to see such a gruesome sight." She seemed to reassess me. "Maybe you don't want breakfast right now. I'll leave the bag inside the microwave—otherwise, it might be River that enjoys the food."

"It was chilling to witness." My stomach loudly responded to the delectable aroma from the sack. I pressed my hands to my stomach and laughed. Truth be told, I was feeling a bit lightheaded. "Give us about twenty minutes to get the horses unloaded and settled."

Grandmother has a key to my house. After all, it was her house before it was mine. She moved across the yard like a graceful dancer. I helped Ella lower the trailer's ramp. "Before we open the doors, let me check on Spitfire to see if he's still calm."

Ella nodded her agreement. I opened the escape door and stepped inside. Starlight whickered. His large brown eyes were glassy with fever. I decided to unload him first. I untied the rope and handed it to Ella. "Put him in the birthing stall. It's larger, in case he decides to lie down." It pained me to see him limping and coughing as she led him toward the barn.

Spitfire appeared to be asleep. I spoke to him, ran my hands along his neck. He didn't resist when I unloaded him and followed Ella to the barn. I placed him in the surgical stall. While Ella administered a dose of antibiotics to Starlight, I mixed a couple more herbal cubes in with Spitfire's feed. I needed him to remain calm until I could get him bathed and ready to geld.

Ella and I soaped up to our elbows at the outside washstand. I longed for a cool soak in the tub, but food and then tending to patients were my first priorities.

"I'm worried about Starlight." Ella splashed water over her face. "The rattle in his chest sounds louder than before we loaded him."

"There has to be a special hell for people who mistreat animals."

She agreed. We discussed today's patient agenda. Ella would handle all the small animals. I could perform the castration alone.

Grandmother filled mugs with aromatic coffee and lifted containers out of the microwave. "Patty and I were discussing the council meeting agenda when Henry entered the café to order breakfast for you girls." She tsked. "Terrible, just terrible. First a murder, and now a suicide. The publicity will surely kill any interest in our town." She placed her hands to her cheeks. "Oh, that didn't come out right, did it? Anyhow, I'm glad I'm not the one who discovered the body. Henry said it was gruesome."

For some morbid reason the topic of death didn't affect my appetite. Patty had sent omelets loaded with veggies, ham, and cheese, hash rounds, and apple cinnamon muffins.

She continued, "Henry said you didn't agree with the suicide slant. Why's that, Tullah?"

"I don't know. It's not like Cody had a bright future ahead of him. Money and fame certainly couldn't buy back his health." I had a very real sense that Cody and Lou Cantrell's deaths were intrinsically connected. "It's a feeling. I know it makes no sense. No sense at all."

Grandmother patted my arm. She blinked at the tears gathering in her eyes. "So much like my mother and grandfather. They had that sixth sense, too."

I plopped the last crumb of apple muffin into my mouth and washed it down with the last drop of coffee.

The food had rejuvenated me. I wanted to change the subject. "Did Dad get the report from the fire marshal?"

It's almost as if I felt my grandmother's disappointment when she said, "Yes, and I don't know whether to be relieved or disappointed. Frank found no evidence of arson. It was as you suggested—rodents had chewed into the wires and not only electrocuted themselves but started the fire."

"You do have insurance on the buildings?"

"Of course, but that's not the point."

I laughed and winked at Ella. "Why, not dramatic enough for the headlines you'd planned to publish in the *Enigma Bulletin*?"

"Tu-llah!" Grandmother's cheeks pinked. She relented. "Oh, all right! Arson sounds so much more theatrical than *rats*."

"What about the fire at Patty's?"

"Oh, that. Just like everything else in Enigma, the wiring in the café needs upgrading. It turns out she needs to upgrade the breaker box, too."

We helped her clear the table and store the remaining muffins in the refrigerator. The three of us strolled to Grandmother's car with assurances we'd see her tonight at the Whitehorse Saloon for BBQ.

Ella and I agreed to open the clinic after a quick shower and a changing of clothes.

****

With the way he was wheezing, I hesitated to bathe Starlight in the shower. I led him to the corral, and while Ella sponged him down with warm water, I tended to Spitfire. He was a little testy when I tried to lead him to the horse shower. While I preferred to have him completely clean, even with tame horses it isn't always possible to operate in a sterile environment. I injected him with a painkiller, an antibiotic, and a tetanus antitoxin. The entire gelding process took about forty-five minutes.

"Ella," I shouted, "you've got to see this." Anger raged inside me.

"Is it safe for me to come inside the stall?"

I nodded. "I'm so mad I could spit."

"What is it, Tullah?"

"We didn't see this before because it was dark and he was covered with mud." I pointed to the series of festered burn marks on Spitfire's buttocks and inner thighs.

She placed a hand against her mouth. "Oh. My. God! Hot shock marks?"

"Yes, and there are too many to count. No wonder Spitfire is filled with rage."

"Do you think Boyd did this?"

I trembled with anger. "Yeah, Boyd and his so-called barn helpers. Bring me the antibiotic salve."

By the time I'd finished with Spitfire and cleaned up, Ella had Starlight looking like the superstar he was. She had also blanketed him and placed extra hay in his stall, along with fresh water and feed. The bath had cooled his temperature somewhat. We applied a soothing balm to his arthritic legs and then wrapped them. He deserved the royal treatment.

Our regular patient load was steady, from trimming toenails to suturing a dog's chest where he'd had a run-in with a wild boar.

After checking on Starlight and Spitfire, and feeding our own horses, we closed the clinic, put our feet up, and enjoyed a cold cola before getting dressed for town.

Ella's expression bent to a scowl. "Tullah, do we have to return the horses to PEP? I can't stand the thought of them being in Hank Boyd's care."

I rolled the cold can across my forehead. "Technically, I can keep them, but there is a process. Due to health issues and evidence of abuse, I can keep the animals for ten days. Then a judge decides if I can permanently confiscate them."

"You know, when we first met him, I thought Boyd was a nice man."

"Just goes to prove that looks can be deceiving."

"What are your plans?"

I pushed from the chair and tossed the empty can into the recycle bin. "I haven't gotten that far in my thinking yet. For sure, I'm letting Dad know about this." I stretched. It'd been an exhausting day. "I don't know about you, but I'm ready to get out of these grubby clothes. I need a bath."

Ella wrinkled her nose. "Yeah, I smell a little rank myself."

"I told Dad we'd meet him about seven. That gives us a couple of hours to relax."

We did a last check on Starlight and Spitfire. Starlight was on his feet. I prayed the antibiotics were working. Spitfire actually stretched his golden neck over the stall gate and nickered. It generally takes thirty to sixty days after gelding for a horse to lose his aggressive behavior. Spitfire's eyes told me a lot about him. He was an animal that needed love and would be a true and loyal friend to the right person.

Like Ella, I had no desire to return either horse to Hank Boyd's care.

****

It was a little past ten when I pulled under my carport. Ella and I chatted about how much we'd enjoy the leftovers we'd brought home, and about the rousing discussion of Cody's death, and who killed Lou Cantrell. Of course, everyone had an opinion.

Grandmother had opened her tablet and showed us the preliminary title of her front-page story for the e-newspaper: "Suicide or Murder...Sheriff to Investigate Death." On page two, she had written an inconsequential article about the two building fires and titled it "Rats Wreak Havoc."

Ella and I left the bags of food on the truck's front seat while we walked to the barn to check on our patients. I felt it before I'd unlocked the door—that odd feeling like icy fingers squeezing my heart. I stood there not wanting to go inside.

"Something wrong, Tullah?"

I ignored the question because I feared I knew the answer. We entered the dimly lit interior. It's not unusual for horses to lie down. My own horses get tired of standing and will lie with their legs folded under them for a couple of hours. My first thought was that the painkiller had relaxed Starlight enough for him to be resting in the bed of hay.

"He's dead, Ella."

"No-o, he's just resting."

I opened the stall gate and knelt beside the beautiful animal. I leaned close to his nostrils. No warm breath feathered my cheek. No raspy rattles sounded in his chest.

Ella also knelt. She rubbed her hand along his golden neck. Tears filled her eyes. "We were only gone for a couple of hours. Maybe we should have stayed with him."

"Ella, Starlight was old. In human years, he was one hundred and ninety-six. There's no telling how long he'd been neglected before we brought him here. And standing out in the rain and mud all night certainly didn't help."

"I know. The logical part of my brain says he's not suffering anymore." She swiped the tears from her cheek. "What'll we do with him?"

I rocked back on my knees. "I need to make two phone calls, one to my dad and the other to the Hermann brothers. Starlight is their property. I can make a suggestion, but ultimately it's up to them how they want to handle this."

"Are we just going to leave him here?"

"He's not going anywhere. It's late. Go home and try to get some rest."

I understood Ella's emotions. In the year she'd been with me, we hadn't lost a patient. Human or animal, death is always hard. I rose to get a blanket to cover this once-upon-a-time superstar of a stunt horse, and I silently vowed that, whatever it took, Spitfire would never return to PEP.

Chapter Fifteen

A gloomy fog hovered over the morning. River's barking alerted me to the heavy sounds of a semi-truck engaging its brakes. I leaned over the kitchen sink to peer out the window and wondered if a driver had taken a wrong turn and mistakenly ended up in my yard.

My phone chirped. Dad's picture popped up on the screen. "There's a semi in my yard."

"Yeah, I would've called earlier to warn you, but I just got the call myself. I'm on my way."

I watched Ella step out of her trailer. She lifted her hands as if asking, *What?* I answered with a shrug. "What's going on, Dad? Who is it?"

"Joel and Barry Hermann. I don't have details, but it's about the horse."

I'd contacted the brothers the night before regarding Starlight's death. A sleek black luxury sedan pulled in behind the semi. "What's your ETA, Dad?"

"Seven minutes."

I was walking out the door and toward the big rig, the phone still to my ear. "Should I expect trouble?"

There was a deep chuckle. "From the brothers—I don't think so."

I called River to me and commanded him to stay. Unfortunately, Rascal hadn't learned the meaning of the word. Ella held out her hand as she called the little donkey. Sometimes we call him greedy-guts because of his insatiable appetite. He immediately consumed the carrot tidbit she offered. Nonetheless, by then she had him secured on the end of a leash where he posed little threat to our visitors.

A man dressed in a black chauffeur's uniform stepped from the car and opened a passenger door. Joel Hermann stepped out. The chauffeur rushed around the vehicle to open the other passenger door for Barry. Now that I see them in the daylight, they are egg-shaped men with thinning brown hair. Each wore a white silk scarf around his neck, gray slacks, and a navy-blue silk polo shirt with a polo club crest embroidered on the chest. Their attire was more suitable for a casual soiree than for visiting an animal clinic. I guessed their ages in the early sixties.

The brothers chimed in unison, "Good morning, Dr. Holliday. I hope we're not too early."

I assured them my day often began before sun-up. "I assume you're here about Starlight and Spitfire. I'm just not sure about the need for a refrigerated semi-truck."

I unlocked the clinic and invited them inside. The automatic timer on the coffeemaker had rich amber liquid filling the pot. Joel smiled as he sniffed. "French blend."

"Would you like a cup?"

Ella grabbed four paper cups. "Cream and sugar?"

Barry patted his pudgy stomach. "Coffee, yes; sugar, no. Must watch the waistline."

Joel said, "This brings back memories of when we were just boys, doesn't it, Brother? Mama made the most wonderful coffee, and we'd sit around the table and talk about our dreams of becoming rich and famous."

I blew to cool the heat from my cup. "Rich and famous?"

Barry chortled. "Contrary to what you might think, Joel and I grew up poor. We drank coffee out of cracked cups and wore hand-me-downs from a thrift store. Mama worked hard to keep a roof over our heads and food on the table. She also instilled in us a strong work ethic."

Joel said, "I suppose you think we're pampered snobs. And I suppose, throughout the years of struggling to make a name for ourselves in the movie industry, we've lost our way." He turned to his brother. "You know, Barry, it's been too long since we visited Mama."

The truck driver poked his head inside the office. "Where's the animal?"

Joel expelled an impatient snort. "Hold your horses." And then he laughed as if he'd made a joke. "We can't load the animal until the forklift gets here."

A large yellow piece of construction equipment rumbled into the yard. This set off another round of barking from River. I called the Labrador inside and pointed a finger at him. "Get in your bed." I reached inside a large container and pulled out a dog biscuit. I explained to the brothers, "This'll keep him quiet."

As if they were of one mind, the brothers spoke together again. "We always wanted a dog."

Then Joel said, "It was against the rules. No pets in the apartment building."

"My dad's here." I opened the office door and held it wide.

Dad parked next to my carport and sprinted to

where Ella and I stood with the brothers. Joel held out his hand. "Good morning, Sheriff. Such a messy business…suicide." He heaved a theatrical sigh. "Sadly, not uncommon in our profession. Some actors lean toward temperamental." After settling a pair of designer sunglasses on his nose, he said, "It's dreadfully hot. Do you mind if we carry on our business in the air conditioning?"

Dad returned the handshake. He held his hand toward the office door. The forklift driver yelled, "Hey, I can't get the carcass outta the barn less'n we tear out the walls."

It seemed we had all temporarily forgotten the purpose of the driver and his equipment.

After seeing valuable racehorses perish unnecessarily in barn fires because of only one escape route, I had redesigned my barn so that every stall opened from both the inside and the outside. I said, "All of my barn's exterior walls slide upward like a garage door." I motioned for Ella to open the corral gate. "The corral gate is wide enough for you to get your machine through."

Joel said, "Ingenious. I hope you've patented your idea, Dr. Holliday. If not, Brother and I would love to buy it from you."

I assured him I completely and thoroughly owned the legal rights to my invention. I trotted to the stall that held Starlight. One shove and the door rolled upward. Over the years, I've learned to disassociate my emotions when an animal dies. Today was different. Seeing Starlight lying stiff touched my heart. Yes, he was old, and yes, he could have crossed the animal rainbow bridge sooner rather than later, but this beautiful animal's death was needless.

The driver called above the engine noise, "I'll let you know when I've got 'im loaded and ready for transport."

Joel and Barry waved at the driver. I motioned for them to follow me into the office. The brothers helped themselves to another cup of coffee and sat on the sofa. Dad took a chair, and Ella perched on the corner of my desk. For a moment it seemed everyone searched for a way to break the silence.

I set my cup aside. "Mr. Hermann, what are you going to do with Starlight? I mean, why the refrigerated truck?"

The brothers chuckled. Joel said, "Oh, my dear Dr. Holliday, Starlight was so much more than a stunt horse. He shined just like his name."

Barry interrupted, "Yes, in fact, he was..." He dropped his voice and glanced around as if he needed to guard his words. "He was...more famous than Cody." He nodded his head emphatically.

Joel continued, "Starlight has won two PATSY awards."

I offered a questioning smile. "Patsy?"

"Oh, yes." Joel elaborated, "The letters are an acronym, and stand for Picture Animal Top Star of the Year."

Barry quipped. "It's not exactly an Oscar, mind you, but prestigious nonetheless."

"I still don't understand where you're taking him."

Barry seemed to enjoy enlightening his small audience. "We're shipping him to a taxidermist in Hollywood. Starlight will then be permanently immortalized in the Hollywood museum for famous animal stars. Tourists, especially children, love the place."

Ella and I exchanged smiles. She tossed her empty cup in the trashcan. "I'm thrilled! Thank you for sharing this news. I never knew such a place existed."

I hated to rain on the happy parade, but I had to ask, "Cody made no secret that he hated horses. In my last conversation with him, he indicated that he'd never won an Oscar or an Emmy. Do you think he was jealous?"

Joel emitted a polite cough. "We've had Cody under contract for almost twenty-five years. His first experience with a horse was with a fractious animal named Big Red. He bucked Cody off. Cody demanded a different horse. We obliged and got a look-alike named Red Rover. The horse was gentle as a lamb. For whatever reason, every time Cody tried to get in the saddle, Rover tried to bite him. Cody demanded a horse that stood out. He wanted a signature horse. That's when we bought Starlight. He was as gentle as they come. For some reason, he didn't like Cody either. We weren't about to spend money on another horse, so Cody refused to ride Starlight. He'd only pretend to lift his foot into the stirrup, and then we'd do a cut-away so Lou Cantrell could take over."

Barry finished with, "Cody wasn't nice toward Starlight, especially when he won his first PATSY."

Noise from the heavy machinery had subsided. The office door opened, and the driver said, "He's all loaded. Got 'im packed in dry ice."

Joel accepted the clipboard the driver handed him. He quickly signed a document and handed it back. "Good. Barry and I are flying out in the morning. We'll see you in about four days."

Joel hitched his pants as he turned back to us. "Brother and I are meeting with Mayor Crow in about an hour, to let her know we're pulling out of your darling little community. *Ride Hard* was to be Cody's last movie. No pun intended, but we were putting him out to pasture. Now with him dead"—he shrugged— "there's no need to remain in Enigma."

I exchanged glances with Dad and Ella. "You've invested a lot of money building sets. Can't you use it for another movie?"

"No, my dear. You see, box office polls show that the viewing public simply aren't interested in cowboys and Indians. And with living in a day and age when everything is so politically correct and the new cancel culture, well, what can I say? The oater genre is dead. We're moving on to intergalactic creatures and outer space. Do understand, my dear, it's nothing personal. It's business."

I sputtered. "What about your contract?"

Barry echoed Joel. "As Brother said, it's business. We're prepared to offer a healthy sum to buy out of our contract with your town council."

Joel took up where his brother left off. "Don't worry. Our crew is excellent at restoring movie sets back to their original state. No one will ever know your fairgrounds were anything but."

The brothers stood to make their exit. I narrowed my eyes at the squatty brothers. "What are your plans for Spitfire?"

Joel flicked a piece of lint from his brother's shirt. "We've already put out calls to other production companies. We're selling all of the animals."

"Spitfire included?"

Joel seemed to hesitate. "Hank assures us he can take the spit and fire out of the horse. In fact, he thinks our makeup people can transform the horse into an intergalactic creature. Besides, we paid a tidy twenty thousand for him. We need to recoup some of our investment."

I grimaced. Anger welled up inside of me. "I'd like to show you something."

When Joel glanced at his watch, I said, "It'll only take a few minutes. Please follow me."

I opened the door that led from my office to the barn's interior and down to the stall where Spitfire stood. After offering him a carrot, I opened the gate and stepped inside the stall.

The brothers gasped as they stepped back. "You're not going in there with that devil! He's dangerous."

"He's still a little groggy from the anesthesia." I made a motion with my hand. "It's probably safer if you stand back."

Spitfire snorted. He flattened his ears and pawed the ground. "Stay behind the gate, Ella."

Ella obeyed and swung the gate wide. I led Spitfire into the aisle and turned his butt toward the brothers. He tried to rear. I held tight. When one of the brothers stepped closer, Spitfire lashed out with his hind feet.

I wondered what part of *stand back* the idiot didn't understand. I spoke to Spitfire and rubbed my hand down his neck and along his back. Tension rippled down his golden body. He blew and snorted. I continued to speak to him.

I pointed to the healing scabs on Spitfire's rump. "These are burns made by an instrument commonly known as a cattle prod. It's an electro-shock weapon used to make animals move along or to behave. Imagine if you were shocked multiple times with a stun gun. Wouldn't you want to hurt the person hurting you?"

The brothers looked at each other. "Who would do such a thing? We've never been advocates of animal cruelty. In fact, we've left it up to Hank to make sure all the animals are properly taken care of."

My thought was that the brothers should pay more attention to what was happening right in front of them instead of focusing on the next movie script or dollar signs.

"Exactly! Hank Boyd. In fact, he tried to shoot Spitfire—and would have if Ella hadn't knocked the rifle up so the bullet went wild. And he continued to threaten to kill Spitfire."

The brothers sounded like sputtering engines that refused to start. Joel said, "We'll not tolerate that kind of behavior. Without going into detail, we've had a variety of complaints about Boyd. Brother and I've been looking for a legitimate reason to rescind his contract. We've tried before, and each time he's threatened to injure our reputations and even alluded to bankrupting us."

Barry whipped out his cellphone and began taking pictures. I said, "That's not necessary. I have plenty of documentation, and as the medical director for animal services, I'll gladly give you a written statement verifying the abuse. If necessary, I'm willing to give oral testimony to Boyd's actions."

Dad said, "That doesn't prove that Boyd did the shocking."

"No, sir, it doesn't. But Spitfire was his responsibility, and that makes him guilty by association."

Dad winked his approval.

As if of one mind, the brothers nodded. Joel said, "We'll see that Boyd is blackballed from the industry. The question now is what to do with Spitfire. We can't take him with us."

I spoke before I thought. "I'll buy him."

Barry laughed. "Young lady, I doubt that as a self-employed veterinarian you can afford the horse. No insult intended, of course."

I brushed aside the slur when what I really wanted to do was reach out and slap the arrogant little man. "What I meant to say is that I'll buy him for one dollar. He's an unbroken, untrained two-year-old that has been mishandled and mistreated. It will take a long time for anyone to regain his trust. In fact, without the proper handling, his behavior may get worse."

I held my breath. One dollar was a ridiculous long shot. When neither brother spoke, I hastened on. "I have a friend who owns the Happy Hooves Equestrian Camp, where disabled adults and children can strengthen their muscles and learn to gain physical stability and self-confidence. Spitfire doesn't fit the profile for that type of horse. However, my friend has recently opened Winning Warriors Equestrian Center, a secondary facility for veterans suffering from post-traumatic stress disorder. It's been proven that working to gentle and train horses is therapeutic for those with PTSD. Spitfire may also suffer from an animal form of PTSD. This makes him the perfect candidate for such a program."

Silence.

I decided to try one more stance. "You can keep your one dollar and donate him to the center. You can call it a charitable write-off, and just think of the—"

The brothers held up their hands as if defending themselves. They laughingly said, "Genius...simply genius! You've convinced us, Dr. Holliday. We'll have our attorney contact you for all the details."

Dad shook his head at me, unable to contain his grin.

Chapter Sixteen

As the sedative continued to wear off, Spitfire became more agitated. I secured him inside his stall, then followed the brothers back to my office. "You've indicated that Cody has no family. Once Dr. Sanreet has finished the autopsy, she'll need to know where to send the body."

I couldn't help thinking that everyone has at least one living relative somewhere. It occurred to me that Eisenbarth wasn't a common name. I tucked aside the idea that I'd do a little online research later tonight. You've probably figured out by now that minding my own business isn't one of my strong suits.

Joel and Barry exchanged lifted eyebrow glances. Joel pulled out a business card and handed it to me. "Have the doctor contact me. Brother and I will decide on which mortuary to use."

Barry looked pale and strained. "Yes, and we'll take care of the funeral arrangements." He sighed. "Poor devil. Between his drinking, gambling, and womanizing…" He sighed again. "Forget it. One should never speak ill of the dead."

But death doesn't alter those facts, I thought.

Dad pulled at his bottom lip when he spoke. I wondered what he was thinking when he asked, "What time do you plan to leave Enigma?"

Joel glanced at his watch. "We'd actually planned

to leave in about an hour, then spend the night in Louisville. Our flight departs rather early." Joel seemed impatient. "We have quite a lot to wrap up at our Hollywood office before we head for Hawaii to begin filming *Aliens in Paradise*. Why do you ask?"

"The investigation into Mr. Cantrell's death is still ongoing." Dad cut his eyes toward me. "I'd like to do another sweep through Cantrell's motorhome, and I'd also like to take a look inside Mr. West's RV."

Barry looked skeptical. "But Cody committed suicide. Why is it necessary to search his quarters?"

Dad spoke in a business-like voice. "Cause of death is inconclusive until we receive the official autopsy results. I'd prefer your permission rather than obtaining a search warrant."

Joel's voice rose to slightly hysterical. "You have our absolute cooperation, Sheriff. Brother and I are still reeling over two deaths in a matter of days." He cleared his throat. "We, ah, the fact is, Cody's RV belongs to us. The key is in our coach. You can pick it up anytime."

"Yes," Barry interrupted, "Cody had a gambling addiction. He'd lost just about everything he owned. If it hadn't been for Brother and me, he would have been homeless."

"Did Cody have a grudge against Cantrell?" I thought about my conversation with Cody.

Joel rolled his lips into a pfft sound. "No more than he had with anyone else. Although he was full of swagger, once upon a time, Cody was a fairly decent fellow. With success, he drank more, gambled more, ticked people off more, couldn't remember his lines, showed up late for rehearsal. Lou made Cody look good. If anyone had reason to hold a grudge it should have been the other way around."

A liar, a loser, a drunkard, and a wastrel, I thought. Not exactly a great epitaph for one's headstone.

After the brothers left, Ella said, "I'm completely bummed. My bubble has been burst. I'll never believe in movie heroes again."

Morning appointments began to arrive. Dad's phone chirped. He frowned when he looked at the screen. "Duty calls!"

"Anything serious?

He merely sighed. "Mrs. O'Malley swears there's a ghost in her barn. Tiny's checking it out. And Mr. Fryberg said someone stole two of his prize Blue Silkie Bantams."

I waved and smiled. "Ghosts and chicken thieves. Exciting."

As he was striding toward his 4-Runner, I remembered the rifle. "Hey, Dad, hold up a sec."

"What?"

"In all the excitement, I forgot that Boyd's's rifle is in the back seat of my truck. It's a .44 caliber."

"Interesting."

We walked to my truck. I opened the door and held it wide. "Mine and Ella's fingerprints are on it."

Dad pulled a pair of evidence gloves from his back pocket. "It could be a coincidence that Mr. West's revolver is also a .44 caliber." He placed the weapon on the back seat of his vehicle, then climbed into the driver's seat. Before he closed the door, he said, "The rifle is an important piece of evidence."

"How so, Dad?"

"I'll let you know once I've completed a slug

119

comparison between the two weapons."

He touched the brim of his hat. I waved and watched him drive away.

After a busy morning, Ella and I had hoped for a leisurely lunch break. The phone rang, and Ella answered, "Holliday Veterinary Clinic, how may I help you?"

She put the phone on speaker. A man's frantic voice yelled, "You gotta come now—he's dying, and Jeeter is choking to death! I don't know what to do!"

I jotted down the address and sprinted to my truck, set the GPS, and barreled up the drive. Visions of a horse, a dog, or a pony, choking, floated inside my head. I mentally envisioned a treatment plan for the animal. Skidding to a halt in front of an upscale brick house, I grabbed my medical bag and sprinted to the front door, rang the doorbell, and called, "Dr. Holliday."

The door swung open. A tearful man answered. "You're too late. Jeeter is gone."

"I'm so sorry. I got here as fast as I could, Mr.—"

"Pate. It's not your fault." He pulled out a handkerchief and blew his nose. "Dratted porcupines."

I'll admit I was a little confused. Jeeter was a porcupine? Who in their right mind would want such a prickly pet? "May I take a look at him, Mr. Pate?"

"Her. Jeeter is—was a girl."

I followed the tearful owner through the living room and out a set of sliding glass doors. I didn't know whether to laugh or gasp from shock. Next to the swimming pool lay a very long rock python.

The size of the reptile caused a shudder to ripple through me. "I'm sorry for your loss, Mr. Pate.

However, if that snake was hungry enough to swallow a porcupine, you might consider yourself lucky that you weren't the meal of choice."

That evening as we all sat in a booth at the Whitehorse Saloon, I related my tale about Jeeter. To prove that I hadn't fabricated the wild story, I pulled up the pictures on my cellphone of a python that resembled a giant pincushion. Grandmother was all a twitter with excitement as she busily jotted notes for her next newspaper headliner.

To change the subject, I said, "So, Dad, did you catch the chicken thief?"

He swallowed a bite of hamburger. "I don't think I can top your snake story, but yep, I caught the thief." He paused, and I knew it was for dramatic effect.

Grandmother scolded, "Henry Holliday, don't keep us in suspense."

Despite her admonishment, he slowly wiped his mouth. "It was little Darren Musselwhite's new dog. It seems like the former owners had taught the dog to steal things like watches, rings, wallets—small stuff that could easily be fenced. When the owners got caught and jailed, the dog went to an animal shelter in Lexington. Unfortunately, the dog, Rob Roy, was never rehabilitated, and now you know the rest of the story."

I nearly choked on my cola. "*Rob* Roy? That's hilarious. What's going to happen to the dog?"

"After the Musselwhites apologized to Mr. Fryberg and offered to pay for damages to the chicken coop, they left immediately for Lexington to return the dog to the shelter."

"What about the chickens?" Grandmother continued to scribble in her notepad.

Dad grinned. "Other than being covered with dog slobber, neither bantam was harmed."

We all laughed.

"Dad, did you get the key from Mr. Hermann?"

He nodded.

"Do you mind if I tag along?"

"Will it do any good for me to say no?"

I answered with a shrug.

After returning home, Ella invited me to the trailer. "Would you like to watch a couple of Cody West movies?" For additional enticement, she added, "I have butter pecan ice cream."

We spent the rest of the evening watching Cody and Starlight racing across the screen. "Wow," I said, "Starlight was really something, wasn't he?"

Ella removed the last DVD. Her face turned serious. "Considering what I've recently learned about the role stuntmen play, I never realized it wasn't Cody chasing outlaws, or riding off into the sunset. Not once while he was on horseback did I see his face. It was always partially covered by his hat, or his back was turned. However, he sure was good with a gun."

I collected the dishes and loaded them inside Ella's new countertop dishwasher. "I really don't think Cody pulled the trigger on Cantrell. Why would he kill the person who made him look like a true cowboy hero?"

"It doesn't make sense. By the way, I saw you give Boyd's rifle to your dad. Do you think he'll arrest Boyd for trying to shoot Spitfire and for threatening you?"

I didn't want to unnecessarily tip Dad's hand. As Grandmother is so fond of saying, *Until there's proof in the pudding, it's best to keep the lips zipped.* "Anything's possible."

Chapter Seventeen

I spent the night tossing and turning, more awake than asleep, my eyes constantly looking at the bedside clock, which seemed to be operating in slow motion. It read midnight. Then what seemed an hour later, it read twelve ten. And so it went for most of the night.

At four, I finally went to the kitchen and turned on the coffeemaker. I had a date to meet Dad at seven to search Cody's motor coach hoping we'd find something that would help fill in a few of the puzzle pieces.

It seemed like we'd been waiting months for the autopsy and DNA results when in reality it had only been a few days. I itched to call Vaneeta to ask if she'd put a rush on the report. Instead, I opened the kitchen door to let River and Rascal out, and I joined them. I looked up. Stars twinkled against a cobalt blue sky. I breathed deeply and set off for the barn. It'd been a while since I'd ridden Gandalf. I needed a brisk gallop to clear the cobwebs in my brain from a fitful night's sleep.

Not bothering with a saddle, I slipped the bridle over the big pinto's ears, fastened the cheek strap, and led him outside to the gate that opened to Dolphy's Preserve. I think Gandalf was as happy as I was for a little adventure. He blew and tossed his head, yet stood patiently until I leapt onto his broad back. I breathed in the tinge of autumn air and felt as frisky as the horse.

An hour later, fortified from a brisk ride, a cold shower, and two cups of coffee, I was ready to meet the day.

****

My headlights picked up Dad's 4-Runner. Just beyond my headlights sat the row of expensive homes on wheels. I parked and shut off the ignition, and Dad stepped out of his vehicle. He handed me a pair of disposable gloves. Somewhere in the background a rooster crowed.

"Are we looking for anything in particular?" I asked.

He shook his head. "We'll know when we find it."

He inserted the key. I followed him up the steps and through the opened door. My eyes widened when he switched on a light to reveal an interior with stunning gold-and-blue décor. Navy-blue leather couches, a full kitchen with granite countertops, a round table perfect for socializing, a fireplace, an overhead projector pointed toward a sixty-inch movie screen, and a wall-to-wall bar filled with an assortment of clean glasses but no liquor. All of this, and we hadn't yet ventured to the bedroom area.

I'm not easily impressed, but I was totally awestruck. Dad had already begun his exploration by opening cabinet drawers. I was really thinking out loud when I said, "I didn't expect this place to look so spotless. Cody didn't exactly strike me as being a neat freak."

Dad harrumphed. "I'll search the front. You search the bedrooms, and we'll meet in the middle."

I opened a closet filled with silk suits and shirts, at least twenty pairs of leather loafers, designer jeans, and cashmere pullover sweaters. I inspected the movie memorabilia on the glass shelves over the bed, all from actors I didn't recognize. There were no pictures of Cody. I was acutely aware of the lack of western clothing and surmised that those items were probably in the wardrobe department and not attire Cody would keep in his closet.

A round king-size bed was neatly made. There wasn't a wrinkle in the blue-and-gold duvet. I remembered the bitterness in his voice when he'd said that he'd never won an Oscar or an Emmy. In fact, it seemed that Cody West didn't exist, at least not in here.

"Dad," I called, "are you sure we're in Cody's motor home?"

"I have the key Joel Hermann gave me, but I get your drift. It appears this place has been swept clean. Keep looking."

I have no idea what tempted me to lie down on the bed. Maybe I wanted to see if it was as plush and comfortable as it looked. Whatever the reason, I settled against the mountain of pillows and felt as if I'd lain on a cushy cloud. I didn't much like staring at myself in the mirrored ceiling. Gauche, I thought as I rolled from the bed and hastily smoothed the wrinkled coverlet.

I ran my hands along the walls, hoping to find a secret door. Lifting the mattress and peering inside the empty storage space below proved fruitless.

I opened drawers. Some were empty. A few had personal items such as a thirty-five-year-old high school ring, a diamond stud earring, and an empty picture frame. Inscribed inside the ring's band were the initials SE, which I assumed stood for Stanley Eisenbarth.

A little voice inside my head directed me to empty out a drawer filled with silk boxer shorts.

Nothing. That same little voice prompted me to remove the drawer. I did.

Nothing. Nothing, that is, until I ran my hand against the back wall of the bureau.

"Dad, I hope you have a flashlight."

"What'd you find?"

"A loose panel."

He shined the light in the dim space while I reached inside. I had to strain my shoulder socket to get enough traction to slide back the piece of wood with the tips of my fingers.

"Anything, Punkin?"

"Whatever it is, I can't reach it. What's on the other side of this wall?"

I followed Dad into the bathroom, which was really a spa with a jetted hot tub large enough to seat four people. A swivel television filled the wall opposite the tub. My heart fluttered when I moved the TV and discovered a speaker box. The face plate appeared slightly ajar. "Let me borrow your pocket knife."

He pulled it from his pocket and opened the smaller blade. I inserted it into the head of a screw and turned. The loosened plate practically fell off the wall. Dad shined the light inside the darkened cavity. I reached inside. "Whatever was in here is gone." I held up a piece of brown paper attached to a strip of transparent tape. "It looks like the corner of a manila envelope."

I dropped the paper into the evidence bag, and Dad zipped it shut. He said, "I think we're done here. I'll have Tiny dust for prints."

We tidied up. I followed Dad outside and stood while he locked the door. He patted my shoulder. "Good job, Punkin. You had breakfast?"

"Are you buying?"

He grinned. "Don't I always?"

As we stood next to my truck, a woman jogged past. It was almost as if she purposely avoided looking at us. Dad called out, "Good morning, Ms. Dupont. A word, if you don't mind."

She stopped, jogging in place for a couple of seconds before heaving a sigh and turning to face us. I was struck by the hostile atmosphere she created. She wore black tights, which fit her like a second skin, and a matching sports bra. The black set off the creamy fairness of her skin. There was something curiously dead about her face. Only her eyes were burningly alive. There was a watchful look in them. Otherwise, she showed no emotion.

She hesitated a moment and then began to speak slowly and succinctly, seeming to weigh each word as she spoke. "Surely, Sheriff, after your interrogation concerning Lou's murder, there can't be anything else to ask me. After all, as I told you, it wasn't time to shoot my scene, so I wasn't on set when Lou was shot."

Dad shifted his stance. "I remember, Ms. Dupont. However, your motor home is close to the corral. I'm curious to know if you saw or heard anything out of the ordinary the night of Mr. West's death."

There was a pause. Her face did not change. She seemed to swallow once or twice. Then she said in the same clear, calm voice, "Cody was a user and a loser. But as they say—the show must go on, so the cast covered for him when he'd come in staggering drunk,

127

when he'd forget his lines, and when he would accuse the rest of us of trying to make him look bad."

"I take it you didn't like Cody very much."

Dominique Dupont shifted a malevolent eye toward me. Bitterness laced her voice. "Cody was a leech. He was a drain on the entire production company." She turned as if to leave, then faced us again. "Before you ask...yes, I'm glad he's dead."

A hundred answers raced through my mind, from details I'd witnessed the day of Lou's death to conversations I'd had with Kellyanne Simpson and Cody. I dared ask, "Did you know Kellyanne Simpson claims to be pregnant with Cody's child?"

Dominique gave me a blank stare. "Who?"

"Kellyanne Simpson, the refreshment lady."

"Oh. Too bad for her."

"Did you know Cody had had a vasectomy?"

"So?"

"I mean if he was sterile, then whose baby is she carrying?"

Her tone turned to condescending. "Your questions are beginning to bore me." She cocked an eye and shifted her attention to my dad. "Sheriff, we're done here. The next time you decide to accost me with your questions, my attorney will be present."

She hopped up the step to her motorhome and disappeared inside.

Dad chuckled. "You know, she's the kind of woman that could stick a knife in you without blinking an eye."

I reflected a moment to let his statement sink into my brain.

"I know that look, Punkin. What's fluttering

around in that brain of yours?"

"Whatever it is hasn't fully developed yet." I grinned and opened the door to my truck. "Maybe a stack of Patty's blueberry pancakes might help. You did promise to spring for breakfast, remember."

Chapter Eighteen

All seemed peaceful and pleasant as Dad and I strolled into Sweets 'n' Eats. The early morning was tempering the heat. Patty's frown changed to a smile. I gave her my customary hug. "Troubles, Patty?"

The bell over the door dingled. Patty sighed as she looked over my shoulder. "Mornin', Pete." She thumbed toward the back room. "You're the last of the council members. I'll join you in a minute."

"Council meetings are always on a Monday. Today is Friday. What's going on?" I pulled out a chair and sat next to Dad. Patty signaled a waitress, who came immediately with a pot of coffee and two mugs.

Patty placed her hands on her hips. She huffed. "The rich and famous, that's what's going on, and Tanti is fit to be tied."

As soon as the waitress had taken our orders, Patty hastily explained about the Hermann brothers reneging on their contract. I exchanged glances with Dad. We, of course, had received the news straight from the horse's mouth (no pun intended). "Do you mind if we attend the meeting?" Not only did I want to hear the discussion, a big part of me wanted to be there to protect my grandmother in case some of the male members got a little too mouthy.

"It's a closed meeting, Tullah. Sorry."

Grandmother opened the meeting room door. Even

as she smiled and waved, I could see the disquiet in her eyes. "Patty, if certain members get out of hand—"

She didn't let me finish. "Don't worry, Tullah. I'll stand shoulder to shoulder with Tanti. It's not like either of us had a crystal ball and knew the brothers were charlatans."

"Didn't the council vote to approve bringing PEP in?"

"They sure did, and I'm just the one to remind them."

The waitress arrived with our plates of pancakes. Dad reached for the butter, the knife poised in his hand. "Come and get me if things heat up and get a little too rowdy."

My grandmother's best friend and vice-mayor nodded. The soles of her shoes made little squishing noises as she walked to the café's meeting room and disappeared inside.

I cut a slice of pancake and plopped it into my mouth. Between chews, I said, "I hope the Hermanns were sincere about paying a substantial sum for breaking their contract."

"They have a reputation to maintain. I'm certain the fact that Tanti is also the owner of an online newspaper hasn't escaped the brothers. Headlines can make or break a reputation." He winked, smiled, and continued enjoying breakfast.

Dad stretched back in his chair. "Do you have a heavy appointment schedule today, Punkin?"

I glanced at the wall clock. "No more than usual, although I need to get a move on."

"Did you call your friend about Spitfire?"

"I did. She's excited to get him, and she's also

contacted her lawyer to draw up papers so the transfer of ownership will be legal. As soon as the paperwork is finalized, I'll trailer Spitfire to her place."

"You've got a good heart, Punkin, always reaching out to help others." A sad smile clouded his blue eyes. I knew he was thinking about my mother.

While he paid the bill, I moseyed over to the meeting room. The voices behind the closed door were indiscernible murmurs. As long as no one was cussing and shouting, I surmised the meeting was at least civil.

Dad and I walked out together. I stood on the running board of my truck and called to him, "Dad, do you think Cody really committed suicide?"

He put on his sunglasses. He didn't answer my question. Instead, he said, "I'm thinking I'll visit Judge Duval."

"Why?"

He peered over the brim of his glasses. "Search warrant."

"You always do that?"

"What?"

"Half answer a question. It's infuriating. Who is the warrant for?"

He grinned. "Ms. Dupont's place. She strikes me as a woman with something to hide."

My phone chimed, indicating a text from Ella. Before I answered it, I said, "Maybe I should go with you. After all, you did say she looked like a woman who wouldn't hesitate to stick a knife in you."

He answered as he crossed the street. "I'll let you know."

****

My day had been stacked with one emergency after

the other. I guess that's what happens when you're a country veterinarian. The sun was sinking below the horizon when I pulled under the carport. Ella was locking the clinic door. I motioned her to the house. My phone chimed, notifying me of a text.

When Ella arrived, she rolled her shoulders as if relieving tension. "What a day."

"Yes, and it's not over." I held the phone so she could read the message.

"Uncle Tiny and your dad are on their way to do a ballistics test. I thought they only did those in a crime lab."

"Unfortunately, the nearest one is two hours away. Dad and Tiny have a recipe for concocting a homemade ballistics gel. I've never actually seen him use it."

"This is exciting." A sound that passed for a laugh passed from Ella. "I've never witnessed a ballistics test before. Just exactly what's it for?"

"Mind you, I'm no expert. Ballistics testing is just a glorified form of tool mark testing."

"Oh, now you've really lost me."

"Dad can explain it a lot better. But it's a way to compare the grooves on the fired bullet to see if they match up with the one used to kill the victim."

"Okay, that makes sense."

A cloud of dust indicated that company was arriving. After Tiny parked his patrol car next to Dad's 4-Runner, he lifted a cooler out of the back of Dad's vehicle. Dad carried the rifle and the pistol.

Dad said, "Tullah, there's soundproof earmuffs in the back seat. You and Ella need to protect your ears."

I retrieved them. "What about you and Tiny?"

"Cotton balls will do."

I sprinted to the clinic and grabbed a handful of white fluff. We walked a good distance from the barn to keep the blasts from upsetting the horses.

Tiny opened the cooler and removed a large brick of gelatin-like goo that had approximately the same consistency as mammalian flesh, though not a total composition, which would include skin and bone.

Ella and I donned the earmuffs and then stood back while Dad and Tiny stuffed their ears with cotton. Dad dropped to his knee, jacked the rifle to his shoulder, aimed, and pulled the trigger. The report was painfully loud despite the protection to our ears. The echo seemed to linger for a very long time, along with the acrid odor of gunpowder.

Tiny walked to the mound of gelatin. He used his knife to extract the spent round. He dropped it into his pocket. Dad doubled-checked to make sure the rifle was unloaded. He retrieved the empty cartridge. Tiny reopened the cooler and extracted a second gelatin mound and set it in place. Once again, Dad dropped to his knee, aiming the revolver this time, and pulled the trigger. I was surprised the blast was equally as loud as that of the rifle, but both weapons were .44 caliber.

Tiny extracted the second spent round while Dad collected the shattered gooey bricks and dropped them inside the cooler. He explained the jiggly mass could be melted down and reused another time.

"Okay if we use your microscope, Punkin?"

"I have something new. I think you'll like it."

Once inside the hospital area of the clinic, I inserted a USB cord from my large screen computer to the microscope.

Tiny asked, "How does that work?"

I explained, "That light is reflected from the sample into the camera lens, which has enough sensitivity for the light it reflects. The direct attachment of the microscope to the USB port allows it to capture and record images stored in the USB."

Dad placed the rifle slug under the microscope. "The bullet I'm comparing this one to is the one that killed Lou Cantrell. I'm looking to see if the grooves on the one I just fired match up with the grooves on the original."

I watched with fascination as the twin images appeared on the screen, side by side. The grooves made on the bullets as they spiraled through the gun barrels came into focus. Dad rotated one bullet and explained that he was looking for similarities in the markings. A minute later, and even to my untrained eye, it was obvious that the marks were slightly different.

"It's safe to say the rifle wasn't used to shoot Cantrell," he said.

He removed the rifle bullet but left the one that killed Lou Cantrell on the microscope's plate. Next he placed the recently fired revolver slug next to the one that had killed Lou. We all watched while he rotated and explained that the .44 creates more force with the same pressure, allowing the bullet to produce more energy at the muzzle of revolver than a rifle of the same caliber.

"Can you enlarge the image a little more?"

I reached forward and made the easy adjustment. It didn't take an expert's eye to see that the striations on the two spent bullets matched perfectly.

I felt myself frowning. "This proves that Cantrell was shot with the revolver and not the rifle?"

Dad nodded. "Exactly."

I said more to myself than anyone in the room, "I can't seem to wrap my head around it, even though the evidence is right in front of us."

I began unplugging the microscope from my laptop while Ella put the items away. Dad said, "I'm sorry it didn't turn out the way you expected, Punkin."

Tiny spoke up. "Yeah, this is one for the books. The victim and his murderer both dead."

I asked, "Have you pulled prints off the rifle and the revolver?"

Tiny said, "Sure did. Three sets. Yours and Ella's, and Hank Boyd's on the rifle. On the revolver were two sets—Jimmy Bain, the prop guy, and Cody West's."

Dad interjected. "Yeah, we interviewed Mr. Bain. He has an alibi which checks out. He stated that the morning of the shooting he loaded West's gun with five blanks because the scene called for a shootout with the villain. Yet when you and I discovered West in the bathroom, I checked his weapon and there was only one cartridge." Dad held the spent slug between his thumb and forefinger. "It stands to reason West ditched the blanks and reloaded with this."

Tiny picked up where Dad left off. "It appears West knew he couldn't miss at close range, and that's why he loaded just the one bullet. We can only surmise that he passed out before he could reload with the blanks."

"What do you suppose happened to the blanks?" I wanted to know.

Dad said, "Bubba found them in West's pocket after they got him to the hospital. Bubba stated that he was assisting a nurse with undressing West when something fell to the floor."

"Let me guess, a .44 cartridge."

"And the four twins were in his pocket."

"So does this mean the case is closed on the Cantrell murder?"

Dad seemed to be thinking. "I'm just a country sheriff and certainly not a lawyer, but I seem to recall that a posthumous trial can be held for a variety of reasons, including the legal declaration that the deceased defendant was the one who committed the crime, in order to provide justice for family members of the victim—or to exonerate a wrongfully convicted person after their death."

I tried to hide my disappointment. "I spoke with Cody the night before his death. He was emphatic that he had no family."

Dad pulled a small notebook and pen from his shirt pocket. "I'm making myself a note to check with Judge Duval to make sure I'm correct about the posthumous trial."

"I'm baffled as to why Cody would want to kill his stuntman. I mean, the night I talked to him in the hospital, he said Lou was jealous of him." I snapped my fingers. "I've forgotten, but when I asked who hated him enough to kill him, Cody said there were too many to count and some of them were as close as arm's length."

Dad didn't seem surprised by my statement. "You're still convinced that our dead superstar didn't commit suicide."

"We'll know for sure when Veneeta sends us the autopsy report."

He smiled and pointed to his deputy and then

himself. "Us?"

I didn't reply. I was going over carefully in my mind the to-do list I planned for later this afternoon.

Chapter Nineteen

I was too keyed up to cook anything other than the frozen dinner I'd popped into the microwave. While I waited for the timer to go off, I poured a large glass of lemon ice tea and set it next to my phone.

The next thing I did was open my phone and compose a text—*Vaneeta, at your earliest convenience please check the Cody West cadaver to verify that he had a vasectomy. It's important.*

The microwave timer beeped. I looked at the clock. It was after eight. Late. I didn't expect to get a response to my text for a couple of days. I don't know why I was so hung up on a medical procedure performed on a certain part of the male sex organ. Except something didn't ring true. Why would Kellyanne lie about Cody being the father of her unborn child? Better still, if Cody lied about killing Lou, it was possible he could have also lied about the vasectomy. And then I recalled his words—*Stage five: a washed-up failure, a liar, a cheat, a sinner waiting to visit Hell.*

After I'd cleared away the remains of my supper, I settled in my recliner and opened my laptop. River and Rascal took up their normal positions on the rug in front of my chair. I typed "Cody West" into the search engine. The result was just as with my previous search—no parents, no siblings, and no spouses were listed in his profile. Full name: Stanley Abel Eisenbarth aka Cody West. Net worth…my eyes widened. How could an A-list movie star be worth less than a few thousand?

I remembered that the Hermann brothers had stated they'd bailed Cody out of financial trouble more than once and had even paid for his lengthy stay at Rockridge Institute, an upscale rehab facility for alcoholics, as well as a different facility to treat his gambling addiction. This thought jogged another possibility. Perhaps the brothers got tired of supporting Cody.

I googled Joel and Barry Hermann. No surprises there. Their biography revealed the twins were raised by a single mother who worked two jobs. The brothers had a penchant for theatrics and both attended University of North Carolina School of Arts on academic scholarships. They were both single, and their combined net worth was listed in the billions. A small part of me wondered if they had a connection to Cody's alleged suicide.

On a whim, I sent another text—*Dad, internet search on Cody a dead end. What did your background check uncover? Did you question Kellyanne Simpson?*

My phone chirped. "What's up, Ella?"

"Tomorrow's Saturday. We have a pretty light appointment load unless an emergency crops up. You still owe me a hamburger."

I laughed. "You'll get no argument from me. Charlie's special burgers are the best."

"Great. My mouth is already watering. Bye."

A little light bulb flicked on inside my brain. I dialed Charlie's direct number.

"What's up, little sister?"

I explained that Ella and I were coming to the saloon tomorrow. "I know business is booming, but I'd like to ask Sally Davenport a few questions."

"About Cody West is my guess."

"You've been talking to Dad."

"Yup. Anything for my goddaughter. By the way, I've hired a new waitress. Nice lady, a widow, empty nester, looking for a fresh start."

"Is she pretty?"

"I don't need you playing matchmaker, goddaughter."

"I worry about you, Charlie. You're a handsome guy, with a heart of gold. You need someone special."

He said with good humor, "With you and Tanti to run my life, I have all the specialness I need."

"Are you sure you and Dad aren't brothers by another mother? I swear the two of you have the same mindset when it comes to dating."

"Hey, I didn't say I minded dating. What I mind is a permanent attachment. As for Henry, well, remember the eagle mates for life." His voice hitched. "Let's change the subject. Tomorrow is Sally's last day."

The tone in my godfather's voice let me know joking was over and it was time to zip my lip about romance. "Really, why?"

"Said she was offered a starring role in some alien movie. She's leaving with the PEP crew going to Hawaii in a couple of days."

"What time is she leaving tomorrow?"

"Basically, she's coming to collect her last check, but volunteered to work the lunch shift to help Vera, the new gal. If Sally asks to leave early, I'll put her off until you get here and have time to ask your questions."

"Charlie, have I told you that you're the best?"

He chuckled. "Sure, and I never get tired of hearing it."

After talking to my godfather, I scrolled back through the notes I'd made earlier. The space next to Kellyanne Simpson's name was blank. Apparently Dad hadn't had time to interview her. I hoped my conversation with Sally would shine some new light on the murder or suicide concept.

I googled Kellyanne Simpson: age twenty-four, single, born in Minnesota, certified licensed practical nurse.

The article listed the names of her parents and two siblings. Being an LPN sounded more financially lucrative than being a refreshment lady for a movie production company. I scrolled through several articles and found nothing about acting credits. According to Cody's pre-death statement, she didn't have what it took to land even minor roles.

I cut and pasted the information into a document and typed her name on the page. I was certain Dad already knew this information. However, in the event he didn't, I placed four red stars by her name to flag the information as important.

Sally Davenport was next on my list. I scanned through her bio. Nothing significant stood out. Born in Mississippi—that explained the drawl in her voice. Voted Most Likely to Become Famous by her high school graduation class. Minor modeling gigs in New York, acting school, and a few insignificant roles in low-budget films. She truly seemed like a genuine homespun girl that had yet to become jaded by Hollywood.

I was eager to chat with Sally. I recalled that immediately after Lou's body fell over the railing, she had rushed to help Mac Harris, the other stuntman, as he tumbled down the stairs.

My phone chimed. Dad's picture came up. I opened the text. *Ms. Simpson has dropped off the radar. Running check on her now. Re: West…interesting. Details later.*

I replied—Re*: Kellyanne, discovered she is/was an LPN. Not sure if important.*

He sent me a thumbs up emoji.

Interesting, I thought. Dropped off the radar? Part of me wished Ella had more surgical experience. Tomorrow's schedule included two castrations—one on a Shetland pony and one on a thoroughbred that wasn't earning his keep as a stud noted for siring race-winning colts.

Now that Kellyanne had apparently disappeared, I was even more eager to question Sally Davenport. I drew a deep breath down into my chest and shut my eyes. Doing this helps me think, especially when I'm trying to recall pieces of obscure information.

I closed my eyes and allowed my mind to drift back to that first day Ella and I visited the movie set. In slow motion, I mentally scanned the old-timey saloon, recalling the people in the room—Sally Davenport, Mac Harris, Barbara Nettles, Sam Jessup, Cody West, Lou Cantrell, Kellyanne Simpson.

Once the cameras were rolling, the argument ensued between Cody and José Pergola, who played Waco Bravo. The director, Sam Jessup, had then called, "Cut," and cued the stuntmen.

It was interesting that such a bizarre thing could

happen in Enigma. An actor, albeit a stuntman, was killed by another actor, and not just any actor, but a movie-screen hero.

"The question is, what was it that Sally Davenport started to tell me but then abruptly changed her mind about," I said out loud.

River lifted his big black head and rolled his amber eyes as if to say, *Talking to yourself again.* I snickered as I reached down and scratched behind his ears. "No, I'm not talking to myself. I'm thinking out loud."

He stood, yawned, and stretched. Rascal, the ultimate copycat, mimicked his pal's actions as well as a miniature donkey could. Both animals ambled to the kitchen. In seconds, I heard the doggie-door flap, which signaled they had gone outside for their nightly constitutional.

"Something spooked Sally, something that caused her to change her mind and keep quiet." My laugh was more full-fledged this time, when River bounded through the pet door and woofed at me and wagged his tail, followed by Rascal.

My mind said it wasn't ready to call it a day. My body disagreed. I rolled my shoulders, went to the kitchen, and locked down the doggie door, then made sure the deadbolt was locked in place. Out of habit, I stood at the kitchen window and peered out. Anything out of the security light's range was a dark void. A shiver prickled the hairs on my arms. I brushed my hands up and down them. I never used to fear the dark. In fact, I had always considered myself a nocturnal person who enjoyed night rides on one of my horses, or sitting on the porch swing enjoying the symphonies played by creatures of the night.

Now I'm cautious—watchful.

Grandmother, in all her wisdom, says it isn't the darkness itself that's frightening. It's the fear of what the darkness masks. The dark leaves us vulnerable and exposed, unable to spot any threats that may be lurking nearby. I shook away thoughts of Earl Redfern and Junior Lampson. Junior was dead, and Earl was locked away for another few years. Neither of them could hurt me again.

I gathered my laptop and carried it upstairs. Just as I was about to step into the shower, the first bars of "Für Elise" played to signal an email. I decided a shower took preference. I get dozens of emails every day, most of them ads from different veterinary supply houses wanting to sell me an expensive piece of equipment or veterinary pharmaceuticals with a new wonder cure for a disease seldom seen in our part of the country. Rarely do clients contact me by email.

Dressed in my favorite baggy T-shirt, I plumped up the pillows and settled against the headboard, then opened my laptop and clicked on the email icon. A big part of me was disappointed. I had hoped Vaneeta had finished her autopsy report and sent the results. Instead, it was from Grandmother. She had attached this month's issue of the *Enigma Bulletin*.

CELEBRITY'S DEATH—SUICIDE OR MURDER?

Stanley Eisenbarth, the mesmerizing actor best known for his role as cowboy hero Cody West, has died. He was fifty-three.

It is with deep sorrow that Joel and Barry Hermann of Premier Entertainment Productions announced the passing of actor Cody West. Mr. West was found inside the movie set's corral, Sheriff Henry

Holliday told the Bulletin. Cause of death is yet to be determined, awaiting an official autopsy report.

Mr. West was born Stanley Eisenbarth on March 15, 1968, and grew up in Milwaukee, Wisconsin. "If you made it out of Milwaukee, you can make it anywhere," Mr. West was quoted as saying in an interview with Glyk News. "You had to be really careful and watch yourself in those days."

The question remains did Mr. West, who suffered from chronic cirrhosis of the liver, commit suicide, or was he actually stomped to death by a wild and unbroken horse? It is a well-known fact that Mr. West had an innate fear of all large animals.

Grandmother had also included a flattering photograph of a young Cody clad in his cowboy regalia. Since her e-newsletter only reached a limited audience, I doubted the article would gain the attention of possible, long-lost, money-grubbing relatives.

Chapter Twenty

I indulged in a large breakfast, two scrambled eggs, two strips of bacon, toast, and a banana, and I hummed a nameless ditty as I strolled across the yard to unlock the office door to the clinic. I had a feeling this was going to be a good day.

Ella joined me. She wore her usual uniform of jeans and button-down shirt. "You're in a chipper mood this morning," she said.

"I guess I am. For the first time in several days I managed to get a full night's sleep without having weird dreams."

After slipping into her white medical coat, she filled her special coffee mug that read, "This girl loves her horses and her coffee."

I filled my plain white mug with its identifiable chipped rim. "Maybe one day I'll find a cute mug to replace this one."

Ella responded with a nod. "So are we still on for lunch today? My mouth is all set for that burger you promised."

"You betcha. As soon as I finish with Mr. Lenz's thoroughbred, I'll meet you at the Whitehorse."

I glanced at the wall clock and headed out to my truck.

****

I'd no sooner walked inside the saloon than my

phone signaled that I'd received an email. I stood for a moment allowing my eyes to adjust to the dimly lit interior.

Someone called out, "Hey, Tullah."

I glanced toward the voice and spotted Ella waving at me from one of the booths. I made my way through the maze of tables and joined her. I was itching to check my phone, but Sally seemed to appear out of nowhere.

"Hi, ladies, I'd like you to meet Vera Jones. Miss Vera is replacing me." Sally pointed toward me and said, "Vera, this is Dr. Tullah Holliday, and her assistant, Ella Sanders." She went on to elaborate. "Tullah is Enigma's veterinarian, and Ella's mom is chief of staff at the hospital." She prattled on, "Tullah's father is our sheriff, and her grandmother is the mayor."

Vera reminded me of a bobble doll as her head bobbed up and down with each introduction. It was difficult to gauge her age. I guessed maybe in her fifties. Although her face reflected a life filled with hardship, she had a ready smile and blue eyes that spoke of goodness. I returned her smile. "Welcome to Enigma, Vera. Do you have a moment to join us?"

She looked around the room. No new customers had drifted in. "I'll stand, just in case we get a customer. New on the job and all, I don't want to give the boss a reason to can me."

Sally said, "Mr. Whitehorse is as good as they come, though he doesn't put up with much guff." She patted Vera's shoulder. "He won't mind if you chat for a while. Tullah is his goddaughter."

Vera nodded. "In that case, I guess it's okay."

"What brings you to Enigma?" I asked.

"I'm originally from Louisville. I'm a widow, a

mother of three, and an empty nester. My youngest daughter is in South Carolina doing her residency in pediatric medicine. My middle daughter is in the Air Force, currently stationed in Germany—she plans to make the military her career. And my son lives in Florida. Unlike my girls, he's still trying to figure out what he wants to be when he grows up."

I imagined a young man in his early twenties. "How old is he?"

"Robbie is thirty-two. He's my oldest."

She spoke rapidly, as if trying to get all the information out before she had to wait on a customer. "I put all three of my young'uns through college waitressing. Thing is, being alone, I didn't feel safe in the old neighborhood anymore. The rent kept getting higher, and the landlord wasn't keeping the place up. I can tolerate a lot, but rats and roaches—nope." She heaved a woebegone sigh. "I'm getting a little long in the tooth, and I can't heft those heavy trays of food like I once could. But waitressing is all I know. So I sold everything I owned, packed up a few meager belongings, and set out.

"I asked the good Lord to guide me to a small town with good folks, and a place where I could plant new roots. Well, when my old jalopy broke down right in front of the Whitehorse Saloon, I took it as a sign. I walked in and asked for the owner. When Mr. Whitehorse came out, I explained my dilemma, and that I needed a job." Her smile widened. "That was two days ago, and here I am."

She frowned. Her eyes continued to dart around the room, then back at us. "The thing is, I'm living in a motel room, and it's expensive. I'd like to find a place

149

where I can walk to most anywhere I need to go. I don't really want a house, 'cause I don't want a yard to mow, but I'd like a place with a little patch of grass—if that makes sense."

I asked if I could borrow her pen. She obliged me. I scribbled on a napkin and handed it to her. "My grandmother and several of her friends live in an apartment complex specifically for seniors. The Sunshine House has a lovely courtyard with flowers and trees and shaded picnic tables. It's in town and within walkable distance to everything imaginable except the Whitehorse. Flo, that was Charlie's former waitress, used to ride her bicycle to work. She recently retired."

Vera's eyes lit up. "A bicycle—that's just the ticket. Thanks for the information, Miss Tullah." She tucked the napkin inside her apron pocket and held the pen poised over the order pad. "Now, what'll it be?"

Ella and I gave her our orders. I said, "Vera, do you mind if we steal Sally away from you? Today's her last day, and we'd like to chat with her for a while."

"Yes, ma'am. I started waitressing when I was sixteen. That was 'bout thirty-five years ago. I think I can handle it." She winked and trotted off toward the kitchen.

Sally insisted that she'd help Vera by filling our drink orders. Once she set the glasses of cola in front of us, she slid into the booth. Her drawl deepened. "What'd ya'll want to talk about?"

I tilted my head and looked at her sideways. "First of all, congratulations. Charlie told us about you getting the lead female role in PEP's new movie."

She tried not to smile. "I'm beyond excited. Mr.

Joel is gonna hire a voice coach so I can get rid of my southern drawl. He says a leading lady needs to speak proper English."

I decided not to beat around the bush. "Do you recall the day Lou Cantrell was shot?"

She nodded solemnly.

"Did you ever date Cody or Lou?"

"Lou was a nice guy, but no. He was in love with…" Her voice trailed off.

"With whom, Sally?"

"Oh, all right. Dominique Dupont. They were a hot item. I guess it's no secret. Everyone on set and probably most of the crew knew it was hands off."

"What about Cody? Did you date him?"

Sally opened her mouth and made a gagging sound. "Good heavens, no! Cody was a liar and a real sleaze. He treated women like they were his personal play toys."

"What can you tell me about Kellyanne Simpson?"

Sally shrugged. "What do you want to know?"

"Did she confide in you that she was pregnant and that Cody was the father?"

Sally leaned forward. She glanced around the room as if to see whether the walls were listening. She spoke in a hushed tone. "All I'll say is that Kellyanne is 'bout as big a liar as Cody."

"Why do you say that?"

Sally leaned forward, this time on her elbows. "Because Cody told all the women he wanted to sleep with that he'd had a vasectomy. I don't see any reason why he'd lie."

"And you believed him."

She reared back and eyed me with a smirk. She

shook her head. "I might be a little backwoodsy, but my mama didn't raise no fool. Of course I didn't believe him."

Her answer surprised me. "What gave you reason to doubt him?"

She took a sip of her coke and nearly choked on her giggle. "Not too long after I'd been hired, he invited me to his motor coach to rehearse lines with him. Yeah, right, like I needed to rehearse my one measly line— '*Look out, Cody!*'

"Anyhow, I decided what the heck. I knocked on the door and knocked again. When he didn't answer, I thought I'd go in and wait for him. He was lying on the couch, passed out colder'n a cucumber, and a whole bunch of beer cans and an empty bourbon bottle littered the floor. The place reeked of stale cigarette smoke and booze."

She fidgeted with her glass of cola. "He'd puked on himself, and I was afraid he might choke to death, so I turned him over on his side. Then I went to the bathroom to wet a washcloth to clean up his face."

Sally deviated from her exposé to explain that back in Natchez her mother was an LPN, and that's how she knew to turn Cody on his side. Her eyes widened. "I have never in my life seen such luxurious digs. I mean even the spigots on the sink were gold. Anyhow, I opened a couple of dresser drawers looking for a towel and a washcloth."

She stopped and looked pointedly at me and Ella. "Can you tell me why a man who claims to have had a vasectomy needs to use condoms when he's making whoopee?"

I looked at Ella. I'm sure the shocked expression

on her face matched mine. There was a moment of stunned silence. I said, "You're sure the condoms were his?"

Sally chuckled. "They didn't have his name on them, if that's what you mean."

Don't ask me why her comment struck me as funny. I was attacked by a fit of giggles that apparently was infectious because Ella and Sally both had tears streaming down their cheeks by the time Vera arrived with our plates loaded with onion rings and burgers on sesame buns loaded with Charlie's special sauce.

It took a few minutes to catch our breath. Sally glanced at her watch. "I still have lots of packing to do before PEP's movers come get my things. If there's nothing else, I hope you'll excuse me."

Ella and I exchanged hugs with Sally. "We'll miss you," I said, "and congratulations on becoming a superstar."

Sally waved, blew us a kiss, and sashayed out the door.

I was almost too excited to eat. If only Vaneeta would answer my text to confirm the unexpected news Sally had just laid on me.

Chapter Twenty-One

Near the end of our lunch, Charlie strolled over to the booth. He set a large sack on the table. "Henry called and ordered lunch. I told him you were here, and I figured you wouldn't mind dropping it off."

I sniffed. "Dad and Tiny's favorite—wings."

"You know it."

I craned my neck to look up at my godfather. "Charlie, can I ask you a question?"

"Fire away."

"If a man has had a vasectomy, why would he need to use condoms?"

Charlie scratched his chin and shot me a look of skepticism. "It depends on the nature of the question. Is it personal or generic?"

"Definitely generic." I offered a brief explanation of what I'd just learned about Cody.

Charlie sat down. It was almost as if I could see the gears in his brain turning. He said, "I can think of a couple of reasons. One, when West had the vasectomy, maybe it didn't fully take, but he didn't want to get clipped a second time."

"Aha." A lightbulb lit inside my brain. "It's very rare, but possibly Cody could still produce sperm. Charlie, you're a genius. You said a couple of reasons. What's the second one?"

"Goddaughter, you're a doctor. I'm a barkeep, a

short order cook, and—"

I interrupted. "And besides my dad, the smartest man I know. Just because I'm a doctor doesn't mean I don't need help with answers once in a while."

Charlie waved Vera over. "Refills for the girls, a cup of coffee for me, and three chocolate eclairs."

"Yes, sir, Mr. Whitehorse."

"None of that, Vera. It's just plain Charlie."

The waitress smiled and walked away.

"Okay, girls, it's possible that West used condoms because he had an STD."

I smacked my forehead. "Of course! A sexually transmitted disease. Charlie, you are the best."

****

I dropped Ella off at the hospital. She'd received a last-minute invitation to accompany her mother on a shopping trip to Louisville. Before driving back to town, I decided to park under a shade tree and read the email I'd received earlier. Excitement rippled through me when I read Vaneeta's name and the subject line: Cody West—Lou Cantrell.

My body tensed as I scanned the contents. The news wasn't anything like I had expected. I inhaled deeply and blew out slowly. I wondered what Dad was thinking when he read the report. The second time around, I digested Vaneeta's information as I read it word for word, line by line.

Tullah, apologies for not getting the report on cadaver number 32547B.112 (Cody West) to you sooner. It's been a hectic week. Attached is the official report to your father with a copy to you. This is the informal breakdown of the autopsy.

Health: Evidence supports that Mr. West had a

vasectomy. Evidence supports recanalization, which happens when the vas deferens grows back to create a new connection, causing the vasectomy to reverse itself. Evidence supports that he presented with stage three cirrhosis. Evidence supports, and was an unexpected surprise, that he also presented with a human papillomarvirus.

Cause of Death: Evidence supports that Mr. West was injected with pancuronium bromide. Pancuronium bromide, commonly known by its brand name Pavulon, a neuromuscular blocking agent that paralyzes all of a body's voluntary muscles, including the lungs and diaphragm. Pancuronium produces maximum paralysis within 2 to 4 minutes. The duration of apnea after a single dose can last from one to several hours.

I gasped in incredulity and continued to read.

Evidence supports multiple contusions over the entire torso imprinted by what presents as horse's hooves. Evidence supports multiple major bones and organs crushed as a result of prolonged pummeling.

Conclusion: Cody West, aka Stanley Eisenbarth, age fifty-three, rendered immobile from the pancuronium, died from being stomped to death by an animal weighing no less than one thousand pounds.

Ruling: Homicide.

I swallowed hard. What kind of monster had murdered Cody West?

Vaneeta had also included forensic findings on Lou Cantrell's bloodied clothing that Dr. Sunny Sanders had earlier sent her. Now that Cody was dead and allegedly had killed his stuntman, whatever was in the report now seemed irrelevant. I did, however, continue to read. She stated that Cantrell had the universal blood type O; hair strand and fingerprints matching those of Cody West were identified on the subject's leather vest. She included that there was no evidence of an exit wound. Which, of course, verified what Sunny had indicated in her autopsy report—the bullet had entered the chest and lodged between two discs in the neck.

I recalled the fight scene I'd witnessed on the morning of Lou's death, how Sam Jessup, the director, had called, "Cut," and cued the stuntmen. At the time, I was excited to get that up-close and personal experience with real actors and a live performance—before the shot rang out and Lou fell over the banister, before everyone thought there had been a last-minute rewrite of the script, and before Dad and I had located an inebriated Cody West passed out on the men's bathroom floor.

I set the cell phone aside and shifted my truck into gear. On the way to Dad's office, the radio announcer was droning on about a new weather system building up. Wanting to be alone with my thoughts, I switched off the radio.

Engrossed in my mental meandering, I arrived at Dad's office in what seemed like the blink of an eye. I grabbed the sack of food and dashed inside. I was sprinting up the stairs when my phone played a piece of music signaling that Dad had sent me a text.

Dad's secretary looked up from her computer. I held up the sack. "I hope you're hungry, Joyce. Charlie sent enough wings to feed a dozen people."

"Good, I'm starved. Go on in. Henry's in a bit of a snit over the autopsy report. I guess you received a copy, too."

"I did. Why is he upset?"

"Oh, you know Henry, when he doesn't fully understand all the hifalutin technical medical jargon, he gets a little beside himself." Joyce made a little flutter motion with her hands. "Go. I'll take care of the food."

"None for me. I've already had lunch." I knocked once on the door. Dad called, "Come on in."

Joyce pointed to the small refrigerator. "There's plenty of bottled water."

Dad and Tiny both stood when I entered his office. I said, "I'm assuming you got Vaneeta's report."

Dad motioned me to a chair. "Yep, and if I'm understanding all of Dr. Sanreet's technical jargon, she's saying that Cody West was conscious the entire time the horse was stomping the life out of him. Correct?"

"Yes, sir, and because Cody was paralyzed he was unable to move or get out of the way of the hooves."

Tiny accepted the plate of food Joyce handed him. He unfolded a napkin and tucked it into the neck of his shirt before waving a chicken wing around like a baton, filling the room with the pungent scent of garlic. "That's a horrible way to die. Somebody sure knew their business when they injected him with that drug." Tiny shook his head and then devoured the small drumstick.

Dad thanked his secretary and set the plate of food on his desk. I nodded my thanks when she handed me a bottle of water. Dad squinted at me. "You never did believe he'd committed suicide. I don't pretend to understand this special gift you have. Whatever it is, I hope you'll continue to embrace it. Maybe one day..." His voice trailed off. He walked to the window and stared out. Instinctively, I knew he was thinking about my mother.

I went to him and placed my hand on his shoulder. "One day, *Etsi* will speak to me, and I'll know where to find the monster that killed her." To honor her, I had used the Cherokee word for "mother."

He patted my hand, cleared his throat, and went back to sit at his desk. "The problem, as I see it, is that Cody was stomped in the mud, and with the deluge of rain we had the night of his death, all evidence on his clothing was washed away, and with the tromping around of the horses and the knee-deep mire, it was impossible to identify any human footprints."

Dad and Tiny were silent for a few minutes, enjoying their lunch. Dad wiped his mouth and hands. He tapped the keyboard to awaken his laptop to pull up Vaneeta's email. "I understand vasectomy, but what the heck is recanalization?"

I leaned back in the chair and stretched the kinks out of my legs. "Okay, in simple terms it means that in rare cases the vas deferens, the male tube, manages to grow back and essentially reverses the vasectomy, making a male fertile again. Unfortunately, this may go undetected until years later when a man's partner gets pregnant."

Light bulb moment.

I straightened in the chair.

"Dad, Kellyanne Simpson, the refreshment lady at PEP, told me she was pregnant and that Cody was the father. That explains the condoms."

"Whoa. Wait. Hold on just a second. What the heck are you talking about—condoms?"

Chapter Twenty-Two

I explained to Dad about my lunch conversation with Sally Davenport and what she'd said about finding condoms in one of the bathroom vanity drawers in Cody's motorhome. "Dad, read the last paragraph of the autopsy under the heading of Health."

After a second, he looked up and said, "Yeah, so?"

"It's possible Cody didn't know that after all these years he was fertile, because in my last conversation with him I told him that Kellyanne was pregnant. He genuinely looked surprised, and he called her a liar, saying that he'd had a vasectomy." I held up a finger to make a point. "That begs the question did he know he had an STD, and the answer, in my opinion, is that he definitely did. That's why he was using condoms. Sally absolutely nailed it when she called Cody a sleaze."

Dad finished off the last of his lunch. He talked while he walked to the bathroom to wash his hands. "I was supposed to interview Miss Simpson." He shook his head. "She wasn't around the day Tiny went to bring her in. You think this woman knows about the disease?"

"I only met her the one time, and that was the morning of Lou's death. She seemed awfully naïve. If she doesn't, she needs to know so she can get to a doctor as soon as possible. "

Dad looked at his deputy. "PEP has already begun

disassembling their movie sets, and the last time I visited with the Hermann brothers, I noticed several of the motorhome spaces were vacant. Let's hope Miss Simpson hasn't left yet."

Tiny said, "I'm on it, Henry. I'll take my sister with me. With Sunny being a doctor, it'll make it easier to break the news to Miss Simpson."

My mind was working a mile a minute. "There's just one problem."

Dad and Tiny shot me a puzzled look. I said, "Dr. Sanders and Ella have gone to Louisville for the rest of the day. I'd volunteer to go with you, Tiny, but with Ella out of town, I need to be at the clinic."

Dad pulled at his bottom lip. "I don't want to unnecessarily upset the girl. This is a delicate matter."

"I'm just thinking out loud, Dad."

"Think away."

"Supposing Kellyanne found out that she was another one of Cody's long list of play toys, and what if she confronted him about her pregnancy, and what if he told her to bug off. I mean, he acknowledged to me that she was a starry-eyed, non-talented young woman and that she'd believed him when he said he loved her. Heck, he didn't even blink an eye when he admitted he'd taken advantage of her."

I paced about the room and came to a stop in front of Dad's desk. I crossed my arms over my chest. "In Kellyanne's mind, wouldn't that give her grounds for murder, especially if she'd discovered she had tested positive for HPV?"

"Here's a thought, Tullah. You said he was using protection. If that's true, then how did this woman get pregnant?"

I had to give Dad's question some thought. I wasn't up to snuff on prophylactic protection. "Okay if I use your laptop?"

"Have at it, Punkin."

I googled several items before I hit on what I was looking for. I read aloud, "According to research, statistically, in real life, condoms are about eighty-five percent effective—that means about 15 out of 100 people who use condoms as their only birth control method will get pregnant each year." Then I added, "Or maybe in a moment of uncontrolled passion Kellyanne and Cody slipped up, and on those one or two particular nights or days didn't use protection."

Dad quickly added, "Either way, this girl is in trouble. And as to your question about thinking she has the right to kill him..." Dad harrumphed. "Who could blame her? I'm speaking not as an officer of the law, of course."

A heaviness settled over the office, lingering long enough to make me wonder if Dad had drawn any conclusions about Lou Cantrell's death. "Bear with me, Dad. We know the bullet that killed Lou was fired from Cody's revolver. All evidence points to Cody as being the killer."

"I can tell by the expression on your face that you're not satisfied with the answer. What's eating at you, Punkin?"

"I'm not questioning the fact that Cody killed Lou. I'm just curious as to his motive. Cody admitted he was afraid of horses. Lou did all the riding. Cody didn't do any stunts. Lou took all the falls. In fact, Lou made Cody look like the ultimate, swoon-worthy big screen hero. It's sort of like the old cliché of why kill the goose that lays the golden eggs."

Tiny said, "I agree. It's something that makes no sense. No sense at all."

"We may never know the answer to that question." Dad picked up a pencil and thrummed it against the desk.

All the hashing and rehashing was getting us no closer to solving the puzzle of who killed Cody and why. I decided to change the subject. "Dad, did you contact Judge Duval about a posthumous trial?"

"I did. He suggested we wait until the official autopsy report was in, which we now have. I haven't had time to fax it over to him."

"How do you think he'll rule?"

"Due to the heavy cost involved, such as subpoenaing Dr. Sanreet, Dr. Sanders, you, and a bevy of other witnesses, I'm thinking once he weighs all the evidence that he'll rule against a trial and leave the final conclusion up to me."

Before I could respond, my phone chirped. "Dr. Holliday, how may I help you?"

I listened to the frantic voice on the other end of the line. "My name is Lucy Dunbury. My dog has been hit by a car!"

"Is he still breathing?"

"Yes. Oh, he's in terrible pain."

"I understand. Is there someone who can help you lift the dog into your car?"

"Yes, yes, there is."

"Your dog may need surgery. I'll meet you at my clinic in about fifteen minutes. And try to stay calm, Mrs. Dunbury."

I disconnected the call and said, "I wish I could go

with Tiny to help set Kellyanne at ease when he brings her in for questioning." I tsked. "Duty calls."

Dad hugged me, and I dashed outside to my truck.

****

I didn't realize how much I missed Ella's assistance until two hours past my usual closing time. People's fur babies are important to them, so it has always been my policy to never turn last-minute clients away. It seemed the two years I had worked alone after Cindi Redfern left for college had caught up with me on this particular night. I'd finally turned out the lights and dragged my weary self to the house. Maybe my fatigue was rooted in stress, or the pace of my patient load, or the mere length of the day, or maybe the lack of sleep when dreams kept my subconscious awake. Not to mention bearing witness to two recent human deaths. As soon as I sat down in the recliner, an immense wave of exhaustion washed over me. I was tired...well, because I was tired, and thankful that tomorrow was Saturday.

I'm not sure how long I'd napped when River whined and Rascal tugged at my pants leg. I heaved out of the chair and followed them to the kitchen. Their empty bowls reminded me that it'd been hours since lunch.

I had enough energy to create a peanut butter-and-banana sandwich and a large glass of milk. After my meal, I opened my laptop to the folder I had created: PEP Murders. I spent about an hour updating the file with current information. At this juncture, I had exactly one suspect: Kellyann Simpson. I also kept going back to the same old question—what was Cody's motive for killing Lou Cantrell?

I didn't exactly know the complete duties of an LPN until I did more research and learned that LPNs can work in hospitals, clinics, and…my eyebrows rose when I read they also work in nursing homes and rehabilitation facilities, and are also allowed to flush IVs in preparation for a registered nurse to give IV medication.

Kellyanne Simpson was an LPN, which pointed a definite finger in her direction as a person of interest.

In a mighty leap, River landed on the sofa. His tail worked overtime as he used his nose to separate the slats on the venetian blinds so he could peer into the darkness. Headlights bobbled up and down, announcing a vehicle approaching the house.

I set my laptop aside and joined him at the window. "Don't get all worked up, River. It's Dr. Sanders bringing Ella home after their shopping trip."

In a matter of minutes, River and Rascal reacted to the rapping on the kitchen door and raced to greet our visitor. I recognized Ella's signature rapping and swung the door wide. She held up several shopping bags. "Mom said she'd catch you next time. She has several early morning surgeries scheduled and needs to get to bed."

"From the looks of it, you had a prosperous day." I offered to make coffee. She declined, saying it was late and the caffeine might keep her awake. I, myself, never had that problem.

Ella showed off several new pairs of jeans and a few items for her trailer. She said, "Close your eyes. I bought you a gift."

I squeezed my eyes shut. "Ella, you don't need to spend money on me."

"When I saw this, I couldn't resist. Okay, you can open your eyes now."

She held out a white mug. Not just any coffee mug. By nature I'm not a gusher, but I actually gushed over this cup as I read the message aloud—"Dirt, horse smell, and dog slobber are always good for the soul."

I hugged Ella. "I'll cherish this mug forever. It's totally me, and I'm about to christen it with my first cup of French blend. If you're not too tired from shopping, I'll bring you up to date. We received the autopsy report."

Her expression turned animated. "Since tomorrow is Saturday and I can sleep in, you'd better make enough coffee for two."

Chapter Twenty-Three

The last thing I wanted to hear on a Saturday morning was my cellphone ringing. I retrieved it from the nightstand and squinted. Why was Dad calling? It was barely eight o'clock. I tried to clear the rasp from my voice when I answered. "Is this an emergency?"

"In a manner of speaking. How soon can you get to my office?"

I sat up and rubbed the sleep from my eyes. "Has something happened to Grandmother?"

"As far as I know, she's fine. This is a different matter."

"Then give me an hour."

"Make it thirty minutes. I'll buy you breakfast."

"Maybe you'd better explain the urgency. This is my day off."

"Two reasons. The first, Tiny pulled a fingerprint off that corner piece of envelope we found hidden in Mr. West's bathroom."

Now he had my attention. "Who does it belong to?"

"Dominique Dupont."

"That's a surprise. What's the second reason for waking me up this early?"

"Tiny and I went to interview Ms. Dupont. It's a good thing, because she was getting ready to leave. She was so uncooperative that we decided to bring her in.

She's hysterical and talking nonsense." He hesitated. "Here's the thing—this is Joyce's day off. With all the sexual harassment lawsuits against lawmen for inappropriate interrogation, I need a woman here when I question Ms. Dupont."

It was the "talking nonsense" statement that had me scrambling out of bed. "I'm on my way."

Foregoing my usual ablutions, I dressed in record time. I did not forego my morning coffee. If Dad was questioning Dominique Dupont, I needed to be alert. I popped a pod into my coffee brewer. While waiting for my cup to fill, I opened the doggie door, then filled River and Rascal's bowls with fresh water and food.

I checked the clock. I was making good time. Fifteen minutes down with fifteen minutes to town.

The local citizens always joke about Enigma's one-minute traffic jams. The one morning I was in a rush to get to Dad's office, and I found the main highway into town backed up with semi-trucks loaded with movie set equipment, interspersed with motorhomes and travel trailers.

An opportunity hadn't presented itself to talk with Grandmother about the Hermann brothers' conciliatory settlement for breaking their contract with the city. All the hours she and Patty had spent researching businesses that would bring much needed funding to our small rural county seemed wasted. I remembered her excitement when PEP had responded that Enigma was the perfect place to set up their movie production company. It seemed a perfect win-win all around. My heart hurt for the disappointment my two favorite women in the world would feel watching the PEP parade leaving town.

Fifteen minutes felt like fifteen hours when I finally parked in front of Dad's headquarters. I bounded up the stairs and stopped a second to catch my breath before entering the main office. Dad's door was open. Dominique Dupont sat in the one comfortable chair reserved for visitors. The first thing I noted was how red and swollen her eyes were, apparently from sobbing. She clutched a tissue in one hand and a cup of coffee in the other. Even with limited makeup she was a woman of beauty. She wore her black hair slicked back away from the forehead and into a tight ponytail that pulled her eyes upward. Diamond studs adorned her earlobes. I wondered if she'd dressed in all black because she was mourning the two deaths of fellow actors, or if black was her preferred color. Either way, a long, thin, gold filigree chain accentuated her black silk blouse.

My gaze traveled to her crossed legs. Her feet were the one oddity in her attire. Toenails painted bright red highlighted her open-toed high heels.

"Good morning." I huffed. "I don't know if you remember me. I'm Tullah Holliday. We met briefly."

"You're the veterinarian who found Cody's body."

"Yes, ma'am."

She stabbed me with a frown. "Save the down-home politeness for the yokels. My name is Dominique, not ma'am."

Dad rose from his chair. He refilled his cup, poured one for me, and offered more to Dominique. She refused. An awkward moment passed.

Dad said, "Ms. Dupont, Tullah is my daughter. She often assists me with cases. I thought having another woman present might make you feel more comfortable."

Dominique cocked a perfectly arched eyebrow. "Whatever."

Dad and I exchanged our own *whatever* looks. I said, "Dominique, with your permission, I'll be recording this session."

I expected another blasé remark. Instead, she merely nodded. I set the microphone forward and pushed the Record button. Yeah, I know tape recorders are passé. My dad is a great lawman, even if he is an old-fashioned kind of guy.

I pushed Play. Dad said, "For the record, would you state today's date and your full name and that you are voluntarily answering these questions."

Dominique answered, "September first. My name is Dominique Dupont. I am voluntarily answering these questions."

There was a part of me that wanted to smack Dominique for her condescending tone. I kept quiet.

Dad asked, "Ms. Dupont, do you recognize this?" He held up the corner piece of torn paper.

She shrugged. "Should I?"

I pushed the Pause button on the recorder. "Dominique, my dad is trying to find out who killed Cody West and a motive for Lou Cantrell's death. You only make yourself look bad—or perhaps guilty—with your haughty attitude and patronizing responses."

A tear trickled down her cheek. She dabbed at it with the tissue. "Sorry."

She reached into her voluminous designer purse and removed a large manila envelope with a missing corner. For a moment she held the envelope against her breasts as if it contained secrets. Little did Dad and I realize the surprises about to be revealed.

I pressed Play. She said, "May I speak freely?"

We both nodded. I almost choked on my breath when Dominique confessed that she had killed Cody. Dad motioned for me to press Pause. He said, "Ms. Dupont, in light of your last statement, I suggest you have an attorney present."

She looked at me. "Please press Play." She waited before she spoke again, then said, "I waive the right to counsel. I understand anything I say will further incriminate me. I cannot live with this burden any longer."

Dad asked if she wanted to elaborate. She nodded and removed a stack of enlarged black-and-white photographs and handed them over. Dad appeared astonished and possibly at a loss for words as he filtered through them. Curiosity was eating me alive until he tossed the stack on his desk.

"Ms. Dupont, for the record, did you just state that you killed Cody West?"

Dominique began to weep. Dad spoke in a kindly voice. "I understand this is painful for you. Take your time, and in your own words tell us what brought you to the point of taking Cody West's life."

It took a full minute for Dominique to control her emotions. She crossed and uncrossed her legs. She trembled visibly and clutched her hands to keep them from shaking.

"Cody West was a despicable human being. He was a vulture who thrived on sucking the life out of others." She drew in a deep breath and exhaled. "He was blackmailing me and had been for more than ten years."

Dad said, "These pictures were the reason he was blackmailing you?"

She nodded, stood, paced around, and sat back down. "Twenty years ago, I was nineteen and full of myself, a starry-eyed actress who'd just received six Oscar nominations for Best Actress. I didn't win, but the sheer fact that I'd received that many nominations for my first major film was like striking the mother lode. I was on my way to the top.

"That night was like a dream come true. I felt like a princess. Mega stars with more Emmys and Oscars than I could imagine treated me like I was one of the beautiful people. I was their peer. Cody was at the party. He latched on to me.

"To say that I was flattered is an understatement. He was so handsome and suave. I was certain he was one of the A-listers." She huffed. "Dumb me."

She asked for a bottle of water. I left the tape player on Record while I rushed to the refrigerator. She took a healthy swig, then continued. "I wasn't used to drinking alcohol. Honestly, I lost count of how many drinks I had that night. Cody offered to drive me home, but I insisted that I was perfectly capable of driving myself in my new expensive sports car.

"What I didn't know until later was that he followed me that night. I will never know to this day if he followed me because he wanted to make sure I got home safely, or if he planned to take advantage of me in my inebriated state. Anyhow, I lived in a small rental apartment in Carmel. The road is quite narrow and crooked. I was driving too fast and swung wide on one of the curves."

She buried her faced in her hands. Tears wet her

face when she had finally contained her emotions. "I honestly thought I had hit a deer. It wasn't unusual to see black-tail deer on the sides of the road, especially in the evening." Her voice quavered. "I didn't stop. I just kept on driving. To this day, I barely remember getting home or even unlocking the front door and entering the house."

Dad prompted Dominique to continue. "When did you find out that you'd hit a person and not a deer?"

She sighed. "It took me a couple of days to get completely sober. It was actually when the police showed up. They were canvassing the neighborhood, looking for a red sports car with a damaged grille and a broken headlight.

"You have to believe me—even at that point, I had no idea that I'd…" Her voice dropped to a whisper. "I'd left a jogger on the side of the road to die."

The features in her face changed. She looked weary and perhaps a little relieved as she continued her story. "About an hour after the police left, I was sitting in the pool, sipping on a Virgin Bloody Mary. Maybe it was the color of the tomato juice that caused the flashback. I remembered the jogger, or at least I thought I did. I remembered hearing the loud thump, and I started screaming. I'd hit a human being…and I drove away!

"Cody ran to the pool. I was hysterical. I was nineteen. My career would be ruined. I would go to prison. What was I going to do? He wrapped me in a towel and led me to the bedroom. That night I gave him my virginity. I felt safe in his arms when he said he loved me, and especially when he assured me that no one would ever find out about the hit-and-run, that he'd already taken care of everything. If you're disgusted by my words, believe me, so am I."

Dominique stopped talking. She laid her head against the chair and closed her eyes. I switched off the tape recorder. Dad and I would wait until she regained enough mental energy to continue her confession.

Chapter Twenty-Four

I should probably be ashamed of myself for desiring an order of biscuits and sausage gravy with a side of scrambled eggs. I'm not ashamed to admit it was long past the breakfast hour and I was hungry for more than black coffee. In fact, I was beginning to feel a little lightheaded.

Bless Tiny. He saved the day, or rather, the morning. He held up two sacks and said, "Glazed donuts, scrambled eggs and bacon, courtesy of Sweets 'n' Eats. Miss Patty said she'd take care of lunch, too. She included teabags, if you're tired of coffee."

Dominique requested a cup of hot tea. She offered a wan smile as she accepted a donut. "Before she passed away, my gram was fond of saying, 'Confession is good for the soul.' Perhaps there's a bit of truth in that."

I nodded, not afraid to show that her statement mirrored my own feelings. She caught the look in my eye and said, "I'm ready to continue."

I switched on the tape recorder. Dad said, "What happened to the car?"

"Cody knew people—unsavory people who knew other unsavory people." She bit into the donut with such ferocity it was as if she were biting off heads. "You've heard of chop shops. That's where the car went. Dismantled and sold off in parts.

"A few days later, Cody told me to pack my clothes. He was excited about signing a contract with PEP. They were shooting their first spaghetti western, and he was the star, and we were booked on a flight for Italy." Her features softened when she smiled. "It was a glorious two years. By the time we returned to the States, I had actually forgotten about the accident.

"I was signed by Meyers, Gilford, and Meyers—MGM. My career took off, while Cody's stagnated, making spaghetti westerns with PEP. I received awards and he didn't. Not only did he become physically and mentally abusive, he began gambling, his drinking got worse, and I lost track of the women he had the effrontery to bring to our house. The last straw was when he gambled away our home, and if that wasn't bad enough, he cleaned out our checking account." Her black ponytail flew back and forth as she angrily tossed her head. "I can't believe how stupid and trusting I was.

"I contacted Ed Meyers and begged him to get me a script that took me out of the country. I needed to get as far away from Cody as possible. I began to rebuild my life and secure my finances. Then, about ten years ago, I received this envelope in the mail with a note that if I didn't deposit five thousand in his bank account, he had copies of the pictures and would turn them over to the police. Over time, the amount grew from five to twenty-five thousand a month, and then to over a million per year. He was bleeding me dry.

"I've reached the age where the camera is no longer my friend. My star status has begun to wane, along with my income. Seven months ago, I contacted Joel Hermann, and for old times' sake he offered me a leading lady role, which brought me to your quaint town and to Cody. To make a bitter pill easier to swallow, I met Lou, a kind and gentle man. We certainly weren't starry-eyed teenagers, but we did fall in love. Lou proposed, and I accepted. This was to be our last movie. Lou planned to purchase a small ranch in Montana. His plan was twofold—to train future men and women as stunt people, and to train animals for movies."

Dominique spoke without animation. I think under different circumstances I would have liked to be her friend. But Dominique Dupont seemed to be evaluating me as a fellow woman, and she found me lacking. She looked down at me and found me less than feminine. I inwardly chuckled. I was a strong frontier-type woman, as opposed to her namby-pamby, useless toy woman. But getting back to the nitty-gritty of her confession...

"I didn't want the hit-and-run incident and the blackmailing to come between us, but the right time never seemed to present itself for me to tell Lou. That is, until two weeks ago, when Cody forced his way into my motorhome."

She shuddered. "Passionate kisses on screen are acting and nothing more. Cody, in his warped mind, read more into the kisses than mere role playing. He was drunk, he wanted us to be the way we were, and he became sexually aggressive. Cruel. I scratched his face. He slapped me.

"Anyhow, even with makeup there was no hiding the bruise on my cheek. I told Lou everything and even showed him these dreadful pictures. I've never seen him so angry. That night, Lou confronted Cody. In his usual sadistic way, Cody laughed."

Dominique toyed with the end of her ponytail.

"Lou threatened to kill Cody if he ever touched me again. He also threatened to tell Joel and Barry about Cody assaulting me."

Fresh tears filled her eyes. "Two days later, Lou was dead."

Dad said, "How do you know it was West that killed him?"

She offered a sardonic smirk. "Alcohol loosens the lips, Sheriff."

"Is that when you decided to kill Cody?"

She whispered a weak, "Yes."

"For the record, would you mind relating the details?"

She seemed a little shell-shocked. "I was very aware of Cody's weakness for alcohol, of course. He never could resist a bottle of Angel's Envy bourbon. And I knew about the cirrhosis. Since he was going to die anyhow, I decided to help him along. After he got home from the hospital, I went to his motorhome and knocked. I held up two bottles when he opened the door. He gladly let me in. I offered to pour a glass. Instead, he turned up a bottle and glugged half of it down in one chug. While he was sleeping, I searched for the original set of photos. These."

There was a slight pause before Dad said, "This doesn't explain how you killed him."

"Oh, that. I left Cody passed out on the sofa. It never occurred to me that he'd wake up and stroll down to the horse pen. Cody feared horses. Maybe the booze gave him liquid courage, and he decided to conquer his fear. Whatever happened, Spitfire did me a wonderful favor by stomping the life out of a most deserving man." She sighed as if relieved to rid herself of a huge burden.

I said, "Did Cody have family?"

She took so long to answer that I thought she planned to ignore the question. "His father was an alcoholic and died shortly after his parents divorced. He had a younger sister with special needs. After his mother died, Cody didn't want the responsibility of caring for his sister. He put her in an institution. She died several years ago. He always claimed he had no other family."

The way she kept wringing her wrist caused me to wonder why after all this time she'd decided to come forward. Cody was dead. She had the pictures. He could no longer blackmail her. I was missing something, but what?

"Dominique, what prompted you to admit you killed Cody when you knew you'd have to reveal his reason for blackmailing you?"

My question seemed to shock her. She cocked her head to one side. It was almost as if I could see the wheels inside her brain churning for an answer. Finally, she said, "In his drunken stupor, Cody mumbled that, in a fit of jealousy over my relationship with Lou, he had mailed the photos to the Monterey police, with a letter telling them where to find me." There was a long pause followed by a half-hearted chuckle. "I figured it would go easier on me if I turned myself in. It's as simple as that."

Dominique's lips twisted into a pathetic grin. "What now, Sheriff? Do you read me my rights and put me in jail?"

Dad seemed to reflect for a moment before he answered her question. "The offense occurred in

California, and since there is no statute of limitation on felony hit-and-run, I'll contact the Monterey County Sheriff with your information. In the meantime, I'm obliged to hold you for forty-eight hours, based on your confession regarding Cody West." Dad pointed to the telephone. "You may call your attorney if you wish to post bail, or if I can trust you not to flee, I'm willing to release you on your own recognizance until I hear from Monterey."

"Sheriff Holliday, do you think I'll go to prison?"

"That's for a judge to decide, Ms. Dupont."

She looked at me. "Is the machine still recording?"

I nodded.

"First, your accommodations are rather primitive. I'm a bit of a germaphobe. If I need to swear on the Bible, I give my word not to flee. Second, and for the record, my birth name is Nikki Lewiki. I was born in Argentina. My family moved to Chicago when I was seven years old. I am an only child. Fifteen years ago my widowed mother returned to Argentina to live with her widowed sister. I have no children, and honestly, I'm weary of looking over my shoulder...thus the confession."

"Thank you for your cooperation, Ms. Dupont. I'll have Deputy Goodbody drive you back to your motorhome." Dad gave her a look that would shrivel a raisin. "If you change your mind about fleeing...don't. I promise it won't go well when I catch you."

I was still trying to assimilate all the information. Dominique was educated and talented, and I was certain she was a very convincing liar. But, how to prove it? "Ms. Dupont...Dominique, all of the A-lister's motorhomes have left Enigma. I'm curious as to why you're still here?"

She hesitated. Both of her eyebrows arched. "That massive monster is too large for me to handle." She shot me a smug look. "My regular driver had a family emergency and left early. I could have stayed in that fleabag you call a hotel. Instead, I've opted to remain in the motorhome until one of the transportation crew is free to drive me."

I nodded and smiled. "You mean you'd rather be on the road for four days instead of catching a flight direct to Hawaii?"

She stabbed me with a sneer. "Fourteen hours cooped up in a plane eating stale peanuts and nuked mystery food? And let's not even talk about using a cramped toilet while in midair." She shook her head. "Really, Dr. Holliday, you need to get a life."

My teeth actually hurt from clamping down on them. I shot her my best stink-eye look.

Dominique rose from the chair. "Are we done here, Sheriff?"

He only smiled and pointed toward the door.

As soon as I heard Tiny and Dominique's footsteps on the stairs, I turned to Dad and said, "Are you thinking what I'm thinking?"

He refreshed his coffee and lifted the box to reveal two donuts—one glazed and one chocolate-covered.

I helped myself to the chocolate-covered. "She believes she killed Cody. Maybe she's lying."

Dad acknowledged this by grimly pursing his lips. "Maybe. She was forthright in her confession. She hadn't a clue that someone injected Cody with a paralyzing agent after purposely leading him to the corral to use Spitfire as the ultimate murder weapon."

"We know Cody murdered Cantrell, and Dominique provided us with several plausible motives—hate, greed, jealousy, obsession."

"Uh-huh." Dad scratched his cheek. "Now all we need to do is find the real killer. Someone with medicinal knowledge."

For the next hour or so, Dad and I puzzled over the unexpected confession. I was getting ready to leave when a timid tap drew our attention to a woman standing in the doorway. She seemed familiar, yet I couldn't place where I'd met her.

Dad said, "May I help you?"

She wrung her hands. "Are you the sheriff or the deputy? I only want to speak to the sheriff."

"I'm Sheriff Holliday. This is my daughter, Dr. Tullah Holliday."

She cut languid brown eyes toward me. "I know who she is."

"You look familiar. Did I treat your pet?"

She vigorously shook her head. "My name is Gloria Farnham. I'm Barbara Nettles' personal associate. She's PEP's assistant director on this shoot. You were on the set the day Mr. Cantrell was shot. He was such a nice man."

"Yes, of course, I remember," I said as gently as possible.

Silence filled the office. Dad finally said, "You appear troubled. What's on your mind, Ms. Farnham?"

She drew a deep breath and blurted out, "I killed Cody West."

Dad and I exchanged shocked looks. I spouted, "Are you sure?"

"No! I mean, yes! I know it sounds bizarre. I

wasn't going to come forward. I was going to let that kill-crazy horse take all the blame. My conscience wouldn't let me."

"Damn," Dad muttered under his breath. "Have a seat, Ms. Farnham. I'll be with you in a moment." He cupped my elbow and led me to the outer office. He quirked a half grin. "Is the moon full or what?"

I laughed. "Let me handle this one, Dad."

Chapter Twenty-Five

I offered Ms. Farnham a beverage—coffee, cola, or water. She refused. I pulled up a chair and sat across from her. "Do you mind if we record your statement?"

"Um, I guess not."

Dad placed a new cassette in the tape player. He pushed Play when I asked Ms. Farnham to state the usual information. "Do you mind if I call you Gloria?"

She nodded. "Whatever floats your boat."

I bit the insides of my cheeks to keep from grinning. Maybe Dad was right about it being a full moon, which brings out the loonies. "Gloria, are you a nurse?"

She reared back against the chair and pierced me with a perplexed expression. "No."

"Have you ever injected anyone with a syringe?"

"Absolutely not!"

"Do you have a background in or knowledge of the medical profession?"

She gasped as if her pet spider had bitten her. "What kind of questioning is this? I'm a glorified secretary with a spiffy title—personal assistant. What does this have to do with my confession?"

"It's routine, Gloria. I'm sorry if I offended you. In your own words, tell us why you think you killed Cody West."

"I don't think I did. I know I did." She said it

matter-of-factly. "I'll spare you the naughty details and get to the meat of the matter. As you've noticed, I'm no spring chicken, and I'm not delusional enough to think I'm pretty, more like an ugly duckling that never grew into a beautiful swan. To say the least, I was flattered when Cody flirted with me. That flirtation developed into a consensual relationship."

From her attire, I pegged Gloria as an eccentric. She wore a pair of red high-top sneakers, a brown plaid pleated skirt, a tan pullover sweater that accentuated her large breasts, and a red scarf tied around her neck. Red, white, and blue hooped earrings adorned her ears, and her short-cropped curly hair was the color of cotton candy.

I was so focused on her attire that I missed a few of her words. "…the bad breath, and verbal abuse." She harrumphed. "I don't take that from anyone, especially a broken-down, drunken sot. I told Cody repeatedly that it was over and to leave me alone. When he produced very unflattering pictures of me in the nude and with the threat of posting them on social media if I didn't pay him a ridiculous sum of money, I made up my mind I'd worked too hard to become a victim of blackmail."

Gloria laughed without humor. "That's when I decided to kill him. Not right away, mind you. The timing had to be just right. When he came home from the hospital, I went to see him. He told me he had a year to live, maybe less." She smiled. "The right moment had arrived. I was about to make it—less."

The rest of her story almost mirrored Dominique Dupont's. Gloria placed her wrists together and extended her arms. "You can cuff me, Sheriff. I'm ready to face the music."

Before he switched off the tape recorder, he said, "I appreciate your confession, Ms. Farnham. I'll consider you a person of interest until we've pieced all the facts together."

She scratched her pink hair. "What exactly does that mean, Sheriff?"

Dad stood and indicated the door. "You're free to go."

She seemed confused. "Am I free to join the crew and cast in Hawaii?"

"How soon are you leaving Enigma?"

"Actually, I'm temporarily bunking in with Dominique. We're waiting until one of the transportation guys is available to drive her motor coach."

Dad assured Gloria that he'd contact her immediately if he concluded that she had indeed murdered Cody West. She hesitantly walked to the door. She stood for a second, then turned back, wearing a contemplative expression.

"Did you forget something?" I asked.

"I'm not sure if you'd consider this important or not. Maybe I should just keep my yap shut."

Dad said, "Withholding possible evidence is considered a third-degree felony and comes with a prison sentence."

"In that case, all I was going to say is that I feel sorry for the refreshment lady." Gloria snapped her fingers as if trying to recall Kellyanne's name.

I exchanged glances with Dad. He pressed the Record button on the cassette player. I said, "You mean Kellyanne Simpson?"

Gloria answered before I could ask why she was

concerned about a woman whose name she couldn't remember. "About a week before Lou's death, we were shooting a bedroom scene between Dominique and Cody. Before filming, I had to visit the ladies' room. It's a strict rule that no one leaves the set when the cameras are rolling. When I entered the bathroom, I heard sobbing coming from one of the stalls. I tapped and asked if I could help.

"The door opened, and it was Kellyanne. Her eyes were all puffy. She had a bruised cheek and, for lack of a better word, a fat lip. She refused when I offered to escort her to the infirmary. I'm not maternal, by any means, but this girl needed comfort. I wet several paper towels and wiped her face, and asked who had hit her. She said it was Cody.

"I offered to listen if she needed a confidante. That's when she showed me a home pregnancy test stick. She was a week past her monthly. She said this was the third time she'd taken the test. Cody had called her a liar when she told him because he claimed he had himself snipped years ago.

"She was pitiful when she looked at me and said if he'd been fixed, then why did he use a rubber? The day I found her in the bathroom was the third time she'd tested positive."

Gloria spoke with compassion. "I didn't have the heart to tell her Cody had given her more than a baby. I figured she'd find out soon enough once she went to a doctor."

Disgust roiled through me. "You mean about Cody having HPV?"

She lifted her eyebrows in surprise. "You knew?"

I nodded. "It was in the autopsy report."

"By now you've probably surmised that Cody West was a *real* winner."

I knew she was being snarky and waited for her to continue.

"We used protection, too, and I still got infected. At first, I was mortified to think I'd ruined my life and could never have another sex partner. I felt some better when I googled HPV and found it's curable. I finally got up enough nerve to go to a doctor. My treatments were successful. For Kellyanne, it could mean that she's at risk for miscarriage."

I jumped with surprise when Gloria balled up her fist and smacked it against the palm of her hand. Her top lip twitched when she spoke. "You know what that bastard did...well, I'll tell you. He gave that poor distraught girl a thousand dollars and told her to get rid of the problem."

"Where is she now?"

"She bought a one-way ticket to Minnesota. I drove her to the airport yesterday."

I thanked Gloria again for her cooperation. Dad promised to be in touch. It all seemed like another dead end when she walked out the door.

One o'clock had arrived and so had my hunger pangs. The office phone rang. I answered, "Sheriff's office, how may I help you?"

"Hi, Tullah, this is Patty. Are you ready for me to deliver lunch?"

"Dad and I are starved. I'll be there in a few minutes to pick it up."

"Great, because I've prepared chicken salad sandwiches on fresh baked croissants, green pea salad, and my special brownies with marshmallow whipped topping."

"You're the best, Patty. Did you get your kitchen repaired?"

"I did, and the insurance company didn't quibble a bit about writing the check to the contractor."

"On another note, how did the meeting go with Joel and Barry Hermann?"

She snickered. "Tanti will have my hide if I tell you before we meet at Charlie's for dinner tomorrow."

"Ah, c'mon, can't you give me a hint?"

I smiled as I imagined my grandmother's best friend making a tick-a-lock motion with her fingers while saying, "My lips are sealed. Enjoy your lunch."

I was on my way out the door and almost collided with Gloria Farnham. "Did you forget something, Gloria?"

"I sure did, and Sheriff Holliday needs to hear this, too."

I invited her in and followed her to Dad's office. He looked up from his desk and gave me one of his *what now* looks. Without waiting for an invitation to sit, Gloria settled in the chair she had earlier vacated. She sat forward, gripping the chair arms as if what she was about to reveal was of utmost importance.

"I was halfway down the sidewalk when I decided to stop in at that lovely little café. Since you"—she looked at my dad—"said I was free to leave, I'd planned to have a bite of lunch, then go home and pack my clothes and close up my travel trailer. For the life of me, I don't know why that reminded me of the question you asked me about having medical knowledge."

Because I'm a veterinarian and animals can't describe their symptoms, I have to practice patience when clients give prolonged details. At those times, and even now, I often wish I had a remote control with a fast-forward button for people's long-drawn-out explanations. I felt my blood sugar dropping, and when that happens I get agitated. I wanted to yell at Gloria to spit out whatever it was she had to say.

She didn't wait for a response and prattled on. "I was concerned about Kellyanne not having enough money to support herself until she got another job. She'd only worked for Joel and Barry a few months, and truly, they hired her out of the goodness of their hearts. She really wanted to be an actress, and she honestly didn't have the chops or the talent needed to perform."

Dad propped against the edge of his desk with his arms crossed over his chest. "Ms. Farnham, are you making a point?"

She stabbed him with a frown. "Hold your horses. I'm getting to it." She drew in a breath. "I had fully planned to write her a check when she said that she had the thousand from Cody and that Joel and Barry had advanced her two thousand in severance pay. They had contracted with a restaurant in Hawaii to provide meals for the crew and no longer needed her. Kellyanne was naturally disappointed, but then, that's show biz."

When Dad opened his mouth again, Gloria held up a finger to shush him. "She also said that when she got to Minnetonka, that's her hometown, she would ask for her old job back as an LPN at the nursing home where her grandmother lives."

Surprise wasn't what welled inside of me at Gloria's revelation, although I had earlier laid aside the information I'd found online about the refreshment lady. Dad's face registered what I was feeling. I said, "Kellyanne is a Licensed Practical Nurse."

"Isn't that what I just said?"

I nodded. "What else did she say that you forgot to mention?"

Gloria sounded miffed. "I didn't forget on purpose. Anyhow, she said she planned to apply for a tuition grant so she could go back to school to get her RN's degree." She brushed her hands together signaling that she was finished. "Now, if you'll excuse me, I have a long to-do list."

"One last question," Dad said. "Did Ms. Simpson own her own motorhome?"

"Good heavens, no. Joel and Barry always keep a couple of smaller travel trailers for on-loan actors or big-name stars that make cameo appearances in their films. They were generous enough to let Kellyanne stay in one."

Chapter Twenty-Six

Tiny strolled in. He grinned and held up the sacks bearing the Sweets 'n' Eats logo. "Lunch."

Built like a lumberjack, Tiny's size made him distinctive. Joyce stepped out from behind him. I said, "It's Saturday. Why are you here?"

She held up a floral tote bag. "I was on my way home from the library when I bumped into Tiny. He said you were manning the office. I sit behind a desk all day. The only thing that gets tired is my brain and my butt. You, on the other hand, need a day of rest from wrestling and wrangling animals."

I was about to object when the phone rang. Joyce automatically reached for it. I vacated her chair, and she sat. "Sheriff's office, what's your emergency?"

She put the phone on speaker and rolled her eyes. A frantic voice said, "Joyce, this is Emma O'Malley. I need Tiny to come out here right away."

"Why is that, Emma?"

"Because that dang ghost showed up again last night."

"Uh-huh, and where was the ghost this time?"

"Just like before—in the barn. I ain't crazy, and don't you even suggest it. Even stole a fresh apple pie I had coolin' on the back porch. My old dog barked half the night. And this morning my chickens were squawking like something was after 'em. Now, are you gonna send Tiny out here or not?"

Joyce said, "I'll send Deputy Goodbody as soon as he returns from lunch."

"You tell him I've got my shotgun loaded, and I'm locking me and my dog in the house. I'm right skittish. Tell him to beep his siren, so I'll know not to shoot first and ask questions later."

"Emma, you're eighty-five and too old to be living by yourself."

"You hush up with that kind of talk, Joyce Williams. I ain't selling, and I ain't moving."

"Don't get so fired up, Emma. I'll give Deputy Goodbody your message. You can expect him within the hour."

We all laughed when Joyce disconnected the call. She said, "Emma's mind is sharp as a tack. Whatever she's seeing isn't a ghost."

I mused. "Maybe it's a raccoon or a coyote that's scaring her chickens."

Tiny swallowed the remainder of his sandwich and bit into the brownie. "Personally, I think Miss Emma is lonely, and this is an excuse for a little company. I don't mind checking on her. "

He set the container of pea salad in the refrigerator. "You know where to find me if there's an emergency."

Just like my dad, Tiny is one of the good guys.

Dad said, "Tiny, did Ms. Dupont have anything to say about Mr. West's death?"

"Nah, she basically reminisced about the different films she'd starred in, and how many Oscars she'd won. When we got to her motorhome, she thanked me for being her chauffeur, got out, and went inside. Why do you ask?"

"She walked in here bold and brassy and confessed to killing Mr. West."

Tiny brushed crumbs off his uniform shirt. "That's one for the books." He grabbed his hat and left the office chuckling. "I'm off to catch a ghost."

Usually either Dad or Tiny man the office on Joyce's days off. Nothing much happens on the weekend. Joyce said, "I have a new mystery novel calling my name. I can read here just as well as at home." She reached inside her tote bag and held up a copy of *Shadowed Reunion*.

I collected the empty containers and tossed them into the trash. "You know, Dad, I'm still struggling to process everything Gloria Farnham told us about Kellyanne. It's not like me to miss such important facial cues in a person."

"You're only human, Tullah." He situated his hat on his head. "C'mon, we're going on a little scavenger hunt."

I looked at the secretary. "Joyce?"

"Don't worry about me. I'll log my hours on the overtime sheet." She grinned at Dad.

I was thankful when Joyce volunteered to relieve me. Spending my day off answering the phone didn't exactly thrill me. "Where are we going?"

"To search Kellyanne Simpson's travel trailer. Even the smartest criminals leave clues."

I followed him downstairs and out the door. My heart thumped with excitement as I climbed into his 4-Runner. Twenty minutes later, he parked in front of a silver travel trailer.

A man was hitching the trailer to the back of a dually pickup truck. As we approached he said, "Can I help you?"

"I'm Sheriff Holliday. How soon are you pulling out?"

"Just as soon as I get 'er hitched up."

"As you know, we're investigating the murder of Cody West. I'd appreciate it if you could spare us about an hour."

The crewman scratched the side of his face. "Whatever you need, Sheriff. I got other chores to take care of. Breaking down a movie set and getting everything ready for the road takes a while. Plus the brothers left strict instructions to not leave this place in a mess." He reached inside his jeans pocket and tossed Dad a set of keys. "You can leave the keys on the counter when you're finished. I'll get 'em later."

Dad thanked the man and said we'd leave the inside of the trailer in good order.

"Do we need a search warrant, Dad?"

"Nope." He quoted Kentucky's statue for warrants authorizing entry without notice. He pulled the trailer's door lever. The inside was like a chic apartment, with granite countertops and white shaker-style cabinets.

I whistled. "Nice digs for a temporary home."

Dad handed me a pair of evidence gloves. "You better hope Ella doesn't see this. She'll want you to do a remodel."

I opened overhead cabinets and felt around. "Yeah, mine is dowdy compared to this." For the better part of an hour, we searched from one end to the other and found nothing. Not even a scrap of paper in the bathroom wastebasket. I said, "Dead end. What now?"

"Back to the office. I need to contact the sheriff in Monterey about Dominique Dupont."

"What do you think will happen to her?"

"She could get up to fifteen years, maybe more."

"Dad, do you mind if we search inside the corral? Now that the rain has stopped and the mud has had several days to dry…I don't know…it may be nothing. Just a hunch."

We strolled through the barn's wide aisle. Every stall was vacant. "Now that PEP has vacated the fairgrounds, I'll be happy to see the young 4-Hers showing their livestock again next year."

Dad agreed. Outside, the cattle pens were empty. The gate to the corral stood open. The dirt inside still bore deep gouges where Starlight and Spitfire had tromped around the night I'd found Cody behind the water trough. Whatever it was I hoped to find didn't happen. It wasn't until we walked through the gate that I spotted it. The gate had sagged and refused to close. I leaned down to get leverage to lift it off the ground, and there it was, hidden in a tuft of grass.

"Dad, look." I pointed to the small orange tip.

He pulled a baggie from his pocket and used the tip of his knife to drop the cap inside. "What is it, Tullah?"

I held the baggie closer for a better look. "It's a lock-tip cap. They're used to keep the liquid inside a syringe from curing and drying."

"How do you suppose it got here?"

I thought for a moment. "The autopsy report stated that Cody had been injected with Pancuronium bromide. With that, maximum paralysis is produced in approximately two minutes. My guess is that with Kellyanne's knowledge of medicine, she knew how quickly the drug worked. Injecting him here gave her enough time to open the gate and shove him through.

Cody would then have enough time to try and hide behind the horse trough to get away from Spitfire."

"Uh-huh, and by that time he was completely paralyzed and witnessed his own death. Maybe, if we're lucky, Tiny can pull a fingerprint off this."

I said with deep regret, "Kellyanne didn't strike me as being that cold and calculating."

"You know the old saying, 'Looks can be deceiving.' "

"What are you going to do about her?"

"Ms. Farnham said she was returning to Minnesota. I'll contact the authorities in Minnetonka. I'll also have Judge Duval issue an extradition order so we can pick her up."

I looked at him and smiled. "*We* as in you and me?"

He winked. "Na-huh, as in Deputy Tiny Goodbody."

"Ah, Dad, you're no fun."

We rode back to Dad's office in silence. I was mulling over the two confessions. Dad switched off the engine and turned in his seat to look at me. "It worries me when you're this quiet. What's on your mind, Punkin?"

Psychologically, I understand why people seek revenge. They are humiliated, especially if they're made to feel powerless, foolish, ridiculous, stupid, or ashamed. All these reasons seemed to fit Dominique Dupont and Gloria Farnham. "Cody's murder was so bizarre. I'm having a difficult time believing Kellyanne did it."

Dad patted me on the knee. "Go home. Get some rest. I'll keep you updated."

Chapter Twenty-Seven

As usual, I looked forward to our Sunday afternoon lunches at the Whitehorse Saloon. Sunday was the one day of the week Charlie didn't open for business. He and my dad had been blood brothers since the sixth grade, had attended the same college, and fought in a war together. Charlie was like an uncle to me.

It was the usual crowd—my grandmother, Patty, Ella and her mother, Tiny, Dad, and me. Charlie grinned when he set a huge platter of crab legs in the center of the table. "I thought you might be getting a little tired of wings and BBQ."

Vera placed a bowl filled with corn on the cob swimming in butter on the table, along with a mountain of napkins. We invited her to join us. At first, she hesitated, until we assured her that she was now part of the Enigma family.

After the general chit-chat subsided and we'd had time to lick our fingers before moving on to Patty's lemon bars, I asked Grandmother about the broken contract.

She said, "The council was more than happy with the ten-million-dollar check the Hermann brothers donated. Actually, the money was more than what we would've gained if they hadn't decided to pull out of Enigma."

Patty chimed in. "Tanti very firmly reminded the

council members that Enigma's crime rate had increased almost tenfold with all the strangers the movie production brought to town." She beamed when Grandmother nodded. "It gives me great pride to announce that the council, with a little convincing, agreed to set aside enough money to hire a new deputy and pay his or her salary for the next ten years."

The surprised expressions on Dad's and Tiny's faces were priceless. Grandmother continued, "And, Tiny, you have an ample budget to order updated forensic equipment." She drew a breath. "Also, the new air-conditioned sheriff's office and government building should be completed and ready to move into before Christmas."

We all clapped and cheered and offered up toasts to Grandmother and Patty for their persistence. Grandmother lifted her hand. "Wait, there's more."

"More?" I said.

"Patty and I had hoped PEP would make Enigma their permanent base. However, that didn't work out, and it's okay because it didn't bring in the employment support we'd hope for. I am pleased to share with you that a major soft drink bottling company has already signed to build their plant here with a guarantee of over three hundred employees. All of the paper work is signed, sealed, and delivered. We'll host the ground-breaking ceremony January first."

Charlie lifted his mug of beer. "A great way to start the New Year."

Ella and I helped Vera clean up and load the dishwasher. Charlie offered to drive the ladies home, and Sunny received a text that she was needed at the hospital.

When we drove under my carport, Ella said, "I need to ask your opinion about something I've been considering for a while."

I waited.

Clearly nervous, Ella cleared her throat. "Okay, you have to promise to keep an open mind."

My early cheerfulness quickly subsided. "You...you're quitting, aren't you?"

"No...well, sort of." She huffed out a breath. "Honestly, Tullah, this sixth sense of yours or whatever it is you have is exasperating."

"Then instead of beating around the bush, tell me."

Ella stared at me thoughtfully for a few seconds. "Remember when you told me that your former assistant left to get her degree in veterinary medicine, and that you'd offered her a partnership but she turned you down?"

Questions flew around in my head, but I decided to be polite and not ask them. Ella continued. "I've talked this over with my mom and Uncle Tiny. I even swore them to secrecy until I'd completely made up my mind, and until I knew I'd been accepted at Auburn University's school of veterinary science."

I opened my mouth, and she shushed me. "I'm not quitting, Tullah. I can take the major portion of my classes online. I can do my residency with you, and...um...I'm hoping you'll offer me the same... well...I'd love to be your partner. Mom and Uncle Tiny are here. You're like the big sister I never had, and I'm not planning to leave Enigma." Her tone sobered. "There, I've said it, and I'll understand if you say no...to the partnership thing."

For a moment I was confused. I'd totally dismissed

from my mind the previous offer to Cindi Redfern. And then I grinned all over. "Whew! I'm so relieved. I can't think of anyone I'd rather have as a partner than you. We can work out the legal details later."

Ella hugged herself. "Let's wait until after I graduate. I have a total of eight classes to do, plus residency."

"Don't worry about the residency. The year you've worked for me, plus the work hours you'll put in while you're taking classes, will all count. I'll write a letter to the dean, vouching for your employment hours."

We called it a night, and Ella and I each strolled to our own abodes. River and Rascal followed me inside the house. I went to the bedroom and picked up my mystery novel. I usually enjoy reading. Tonight I couldn't concentrate. This had been a strange week. Yesterday had been even more abnormal, with two women confessing to killing the same man. The lines on the page blurred together until, mercifully, my eyelids grew heavy and I drifted off to sleep.

****

I awoke smiling. It took me a second to remember why, but then I remembered and grinned all over. Ella was going back to school to finish her degree, and then she and I would form a partnership, and perhaps hire an assistant. I thought how wonderful it would be to take a vacation. In fact, since opening my practice, I'd never had time for that kind of fun.

I was enjoying my second cup of coffee and browsing through a new veterinary medicine journal for bioscience and biosafety when my phone rang twice. The number on my caller ID was from my answering service.

"This is Tullah, what's up, Gayle?"

Her voice sounded a little breathless. "A Mr. Larry North said one of his bison bulls managed to actually climb over a six-foot pen to get in with another bull. I guess it's a bloody mess and you need to get there asap. He said to bring a tranquilizer gun."

She gave me the address. I called Ella and explained the situation. "I don't know how long this will take. Whether or not I need to put him down will depend on how badly injured the bovine is."

"Don't worry, Tullah. All of our appointments today are with small animals. If I run into any problems I can't handle, I'll call you. In the meantime, be careful. Bison bulls are aggressive and very dangerous."

I unplugged the coffeemaker and made sure to lock the kitchen door. I raced to my truck, and as I drove up the driveway, I thought how lucky I am to have such an interesting and sometimes dangerous profession.

Chapter Twenty-Eight

The week flew by in a hop, skip, and a jump. I hadn't heard from Dad and was curious to know if he'd had any news from the Monterey sheriff and what his plans were for traveling to Minnesota.

It was late Friday, and I was in desperate need for groceries. A sudden deluge of rain pelted my windshield as I left my driveway and pulled onto the road to town. Through the rhythmic slash of my wipers, a memory flashed in my mind's eye—three slash marks and blood. I couldn't quite bring the recollection into focus. Instead, I concentrated on the road. I almost heard Dad's voice reminding me to drive safely and not to speed.

The rain was still falling heavily, and it was after six when I parked in front of his office. I sent him a text letting him know I was outside. Lightning coursed across the sky. This storm was going to be a humdinger. I reached over the back seat for my umbrella. By the time I'd opened it and stepped out of the truck, Dad stood with the office door open.

"Why aren't you safe at home instead of driving in a storm?"

I followed him up the stairs to his office. "Don't scold, Dad. I'm a safe driver, and besides I need to grocery shop. I thought I'd visit with you first."

"If this storm doesn't let up, you may have to sleep

on my sofa tonight and do your shopping tomorrow."

"Would you mind terribly having me as a guest?"

He folded me into his arms. "I don't mean to be crotchety. How about a cola and some leftover potato salad?"

I grinned. "You know me. I never turn down food." I decided to ease into my questions about Dominique and Gloria. "Did Tiny find Mrs. O'Malley's ghost?"

Dad removed his boots and wiggled his toes. Enigma is like most small rural towns—the sidewalks roll up after six, and earlier when it's storming. He stretched his long legs and yawned. Then he thumbed toward the closed door that hid the jail cells. "Ghosts don't eat apple pie, but a hungry prison escapee does. Tiny caught the man asleep in Emma's hayloft. His name is Baler Everston, and he's not altogether harmless. He was incarcerated for vandalizing several churches and stealing from the offering plates. He's also bi-polar and off his meds. I'm holding him until a deputy from Jefferson County can come get him."

"That's scary, Dad. Bi-polar, he could have harmed or maybe even killed Mrs. O'Malley."

"Yep, Emma was pretty shaken up, hopefully enough to sell the farm and move into town."

"What about the first time Tiny went to the farm? Was this bi-polar guy hiding in the barn then, too?"

Dad chuckled. "No, Emma was a little embarrassed when she admitted that it was the night of the full moon. She'd apparently hung out a sheet to dry and had forgotten to take it down. She discovered her not-so-ghostly apparition hanging on the clothesline the next morning."

"Poor Mrs. O'Malley. I'd be glad if she's deciding

to move to town." I smiled. "To change the subject, it's been a week. Have you heard from Monterey?"

He scratched his head. "You know the saying about weaving a wicked web in order to deceive…I'm telling you, Punkin, this Cody West case is filled with a plethora of deceit."

I shoveled in a spoonful of potato salad. "How so?"

A file folder lay on his desk. He flipped it open. "This is an email from Sheriff Orlando Ramos." Dad handed me a lengthy email and said, "Skip over the introduction and thank you for your interest, et cetera, and read it aloud."

I moistened my throat with a swig of cola. "Based on your information, my department of investigations thoroughly searched records dating back twenty years to amply cover the estimated time of cases to include the alleged hit-and-run, and your person of interest's recent declaration of guilt.

"While our officer did locate files of several fatalities, and a few hundred non-fatal crashes involving vehicles with deer and coyote, no record of a hit-and-run involving a jogger or bicyclist was located. We did have our forensic photographer enhance the photos you attached with your query. As a leading expert in digital forensics and image analysis, he scrutinized them for the almost imperceptible signs that suggest the image had been manipulated. It appears the photos you sent have been tampered with. The telltale signs don't jump out at you. Although these are black-and-white photos, according to our expert these prints are littered with evidence—the shadows do not match up. The location, size, and color of the reflections tell us about the location, size, and color of the light source. Our expert concludes that these photos were not taken in Monterey. The trees and surrounding foliage are not indicative of our area. In fact, our expert suggests these photos were not shot anywhere in California.

"We ran the names Dominique Dupont and Nikki Lewiki through multiple databases. She is clean. Not even a parking ticket. Cody West aka Stanley Eisenbarth has an extensive rap sheet—extortion, drunk and disorderly, soliciting drugs—to name a few.

"Our conclusion: It appears Ms. Dupont was either duped into thinking she had committed a crime or was a victim of a terrible hoax. If we can be of further service, please do not hesitate to contact my office."

I knew my mouth was gaped open wide enough to catch flies. "Un. Be. Liev. Able! It's totally obvious that Cody was as slimy as all our witnesses have claimed. I'm utterly astounded that Dominique paid millions of dollars in blackmail and for what…a bunch of fake pictures."

I was still holding the email when Tiny entered the office and hung his hat on the rack. He chuckled. "Big surprise, huh, Tullah."

I placed the message on top of the manila folder. "If I were her, I'd want to commit murder, too."

"I've been a deputy for almost twenty years. People never cease to amaze me." He removed his weapon and placed it inside the bottom drawer of Dad's desk. "The thing I can't figure is why the women would confess to committing a crime knowing full well they could face prison time."

We both looked at my dad. He'd always been a student of law. In my mind, he would have made an excellent prosecuting attorney, except he preferred wearing a badge to being gussied up in a suit and tie.

"Dad?" I prompted when he didn't reply right away.

He gestured toward the computer. "I'm sure you'd find a more accurate answer if you researched it."

Tiny lowered his hulk into a chair. "C'mon, Henry, be a sport and humor us."

I knew Dad didn't mind having his ego fanned a tad. He grunted. "There are several reasons why people confess to crimes they didn't commit. These are sometimes called compliant false confessions. People confess voluntarily to attract attention to gain popularity. Other times, they might feel pressured to confess because they want to avoid a harsher sentence. On occasion, police will tell a suspect that the evidence is so strong they're going to be convicted no matter what, but if they provide a confession their sentence will be more lenient. And sometimes a person confesses to a crime they didn't commit to protect a third party."

Tiny shook his head at this information. "It seems incredible that innocent people would incriminate themselves by confessing to something they didn't actually do."

I thought for a moment. "Maybe Dominique felt trapped, like she had no way out. And maybe she and Gloria internalized their confessions to the point of convincing themselves they were guilty."

Tiny mimicked Dad by stretching his long legs. "Makes sense to me."

I looked at Tiny. "Were you able to pull a print off the lock cap?"

"Sorry, whoever popped West with the needle must've worn gloves. It's my shift." He thumbed toward the closed door. "How's our prisoner?"

Dad tugged on his boots. "A lot calmer since Sunny coaxed him into taking his medication. We'll be rid of him tomorrow."

Dad motioned me to follow him. "C'mon on, Punkin. The weather is getting worse. The best I can fix you is a grilled cheese sandwich and a bowl of tomato soup."

I followed Dad upstairs to his loft apartment and helped him prepare our supper. "Did you contact law enforcement in Minnetonka?"

"Not yet."

"Why are you holding off?"

He raised an eyebrow. "I was waiting to hear from Monterey. I'll touch base with Judge Duvall in the morning about the extradition order."

I dipped my sandwich into the soup and enjoyed the bite. "This case is like a big puzzle with several of the pieces missing. I can understand why Cody blackmailed Dominique—to keep his empty pockets filled, and I can understand that she was gullible enough to fall for the fake pictures, and why she paid Cody to keep him quiet."

I felt myself slip into a sort of dreamlike state where I wandered around inside my mind searching for those missing puzzle pieces.

"Punk...Punkin...Tullah?" Dad snapped his fingers in front of my face. "Where'd you go?"

Exasperation rode over me like a storm cloud. *Think.* Frustrated, I rubbed my temples.

"It's right there, Dad, right in front of me. I just can't grab hold of it."

"Grab hold of what, Tullah?"

Be it incorrigible animal or human, I had never backed away from a challenge. "The truth."

Lightning lit up the room, followed by a heavy volley of thunder that vibrated the hundred-year-old building. The lights flickered, and for a couple of seconds we were in the dark before the power came back on.

Dad said, "It'd make me feel a whole lot better if you stayed the night. You can have my bed, and I'll take the sofa."

I live alone in the same two-story house in which I was born. My house is filled with happy and sad memories. I can look out the kitchen window and feel pride that I converted the old barn into a thriving clinic and animal hospital, and that I have the privilege of living and working where I was born.

I have never been truly afraid of being alone or of things that go bump in the night…not until, on separate occasions, two depraved men broke into my home and tried to kill me. The older I get, the more cautious I become.

My entire life, I have been in tune with the spirit world. My grandmother says I have an inborn temperament, that even before I was born I was chosen to be an empath. She claims she saw it the moment I came out of the womb. It's true, I am more responsive to light, smells, touch, movement, temperature, and sound than most people.

Grandmother calls my empathic abilities a gift. I call it a curse because the voices and the faces visit in my dreams, often leaving me exhausted and unsettled and leading places I prefer not to go.

Perhaps because I was wrapped in his overly large

T-shirt and snuggled under the covers in his bed, and perhaps because my dad was asleep in the next room, I felt safe. Tonight there were no dreams and no voices. I closed my eyes, and when I opened them, morning had arrived.

Chapter Twenty-Nine

The aroma of frying bacon woke me. I stretched and rubbed sleep from my eyes. Maybe it was because my brain was rested that, clear as day, the missing pieces of the puzzle had fallen into place.

I scrambled from bed, took a quick shower, dressed, and joined Dad for breakfast. After a few minutes of small talk, I said, "I know who killed Cody."

He joined me at the table. "I'm all ears."

I filled him in.

Dad spoke kindly and with a modicum of tolerance. "You know the evidence suggests both women are innocent."

"Yes, sir. I also know in the mystery books the real killer is always the most unlikely person. But that plot point rarely applies to real life. So often the obvious truth is right in front of us."

"So you don't believe Kellyanne was in on the murder?"

"No. She had nothing to gain by killing him."

"I'm listening. What's your theory?"

"I believe Dominique became suspicious about the authenticity of the photos. She may have confided in Gloria about her suspicion. Gloria had her own score to settle with Cody. The two of them decided to take matters into their own hands."

I proposed that we set a trap. If the plan worked,

case solved. If the entire set-up went awry—nothing ventured, nothing gained.

He stared at me a moment as if I had lost my mind. I don't know how long I'd sat there—only a few minutes in reality, I suppose, before he said, "It just might work."

I made one very important phone call. I put the phone on speaker. The conversation was short. The voice on the other end said, "Yes, and thank you."

****

It seemed like an eternity before Tiny arrived. When the door opened, Dad and I turned, and Tiny escorted Dominique and Gloria into Dad's office and motioned for them to sit.

While waiting for their arrival, Dad had cleared his desk. I had carefully created a display to include the orange lock cap we'd found at the corral, an empty syringe from my clinic, a pair of soiled rubber gloves, a wadded piece of paper, and the emailed message from Monterey.

Dad forewent his normal courtesy and directed Gloria and Dominique to sit. Body language in both humans and animals speak volumes. Lines of tension marred both women's faces. Dominique perched on the edge of the chair like a bird ready for flight. Gloria's right knee bounced up and down.

I deliberately walked to the desk and picked up the syringe and toyed with it. Then I set the orange cap over the needle. A perfect fit. I casually used my thumb to flip it up, allowing the cap to drop to the floor. I couldn't have planned it more perfectly when the cap rolled and settled in front of Dominique's shoe.

Her eyes widened. She clasped her hands together

and slid back into the chair. She rolled her tongue over her ruby-red lips. "Your deputy said you had news from Monterey."

Dad reached for the email and handed it to her along with the pictures. Her eyes darted back and forth as she read, and when she'd finished, she closed her eyes and drew in a deep breath.

Gloria asked, "What does it say?"

Dominique hesitated a second. Her voice was deadpan. "All these years of paying that slimy, booze-guzzling, skirt-chasing bastard, and for what—fake pictures." She loosed a hysterical cackle and, with the pictures in hand, leapt from the chair.

She ripped them into pieces and tossed them in the air like confetti and continued to laugh. Tiny filled a glass with water. He led Dominique to the chair and helped her sit down.

Gloria snorted impatiently. "At least that's cleared up." She stood. "Since we didn't really kill Cody, are we free to go? Dominique and I have a plane to catch."

The tension in the room was broken by a loud pecking at the window. Tiny looked at me and said, "Tullah?"

Dominique drew back as a crow continued its rhythmic tapping against the glass pane. She placed her hands over her ears. Panic laced her voice. "Make it stop."

My smile was hidden when I walked to the window. I placed my hand against the pane and in Cherokee whispered my thanks to the crow for visiting to let me know our cleverness and teamwork would cause two shrewd criminals to convict themselves.

I turned to face the women. "Most Native

Americans believe the crow is a spirit animal with psychic abilities. He knows there is a liar amongst us."

Two liars to be exact.

Gloria's leg continued to jiggle up and down. "Bunch of mumbo-jumbo, if you ask me."

Some magnetism impelled me to lift the paper wad from our little display. I made a production of unfolding it and smoothing it out. There is a one-hour difference between Minnetonka and Enigma. I prayed for the phone to ring.

I cleared my throat when Dad shot me his famous *what now* look. Dominique and Gloria's eyes were riveted on the wrinkled notebook paper. I smiled an indulgent smile and sighed with inner relief when the phone rang.

Dad answered, "Sheriff's office. Sheriff Holliday speaking."

He listened.

"Yes, everyone is here. I'll put you on speaker."

Silence.

Dad said, "Ms. Dupont…Ms. Farnham, I'm sure you remember Kellyanne Simpson."

Panic lit Dominique and Gloria's eyes.

Dad said, "Ms. Simpson, in your own words, would you mind repeating what you told me last night?"

"Of course, Sheriff Holliday."

"With your permission may I record this conversation?"

"Yes, sir."

"Then for the record, please state your name, today's date, and that you are volunteering this information."

Kellyanne complied.

We heard her clear her throat. She said, "Forgive me if my voice cracks. I'm a little nervous."

I said, "You are safe, Kellyanne. They can't hurt you now."

She spoke clearly. "The night of Cody's death, I had planned to kill myself. I was pregnant by a man who said I wasn't worth his time; worse, he gave me a disease. I'd received severance notice, and yes, two thousand dollars is a lot of money, but not enough to pay for my grandmother's continued nursing care. I was unemployed and desperate. I couldn't take care of her, me, and a baby.

"I knew Cody kept all kinds of drugs. I'd planned to visit him and steal enough pills to put me to sleep forever. Believe me, it took hours for me to work up enough courage to walk to his motorhome.

"It was a little after two in the morning. The rain was coming down heavy, but I didn't care. I guess at that point I was sort of emotionally numb. Anyhow, as I rounded the corner of Dominique's coach, I spotted her and Gloria. They had Cody between them. I knew the way his feet dragged that he was either drunk or unconscious.

"I decided to follow and stayed in the shadows. I hid inside an empty stall closest to the rear barn door and watched as they struggled to drag Cody outside to the corral."

There was a pause.

Dad asked, "What else did you see, Kellyanne?"

"I...I saw Gloria open the corral gate. Cody sagged to the ground. She helped Dominique hold him up and then drag him to the horse trough. That's when

Dominique lifted Cody's shirt and jabbed him with a needle."

Dominique yelled, "She's lying! She killed him. Gloria told you Kellyanne is a nurse. She'll do anything to save herself!"

Dad ordered Dominique to be quiet. He said, "Kellyanne, it was dark that night. There was no moon. How were you able to see Ms. Dupont inject Mr. West with a syringe?"

There was an audible sob. "Because Gloria had a flashlight. She held it so Dominique could see. She injected him on the left side close to his heart."

Dad asked, "Where were the horses?"

"Inside the barn. Gloria and Dominique shoved back the rear doors that open to the outside stock pens. Then, after Gloria led Starlight out of his stall and into the corral, she hid behind the gate, apparently to protect herself. Dominique opened Spitfire's stall. She waved her arms and screamed at the horse. I guess it startled him, because he raced after Starlight. When he got to the corral, he first reared and then lashed out with his hind legs. I thought he'd struck Gloria. Anyhow, Dominique raced forward yelling until Spitfire ran all the way into the pen. That's when she and Gloria hurried and shut the gate to the corral. By this time the rain was coming down in sheets, and they both sprinted toward the barn.

"I was so scared I decided to run back to my trailer, except I was a little too hasty, and they saw me. Gloria grabbed me, we struggled, and she hit me in the face with her fist. Dominique said she had more syringes, and if I knew what was good for me I'd better keep my mouth shut."

Dad's eyes took on a steely shine at the confession. I understood how he felt.

"Kellyanne, this is Tullah. Earlier, Gloria stated that she found you in the ladies' room. You were crying and said Cody had hit you. Did that happen?"

"Well, yes and no. She did give me comfort in the bathroom, but Cody never hit me. He gave me a thousand dollars and told me to get rid of the problem."

Dominique's grin turned slightly wicked. She pierced me with a stabbing gaze. Gloria on the other hand looked as if she had just awakened from a deep sleep and was struggling to process the direness of her situation.

Dominique pointed toward Gloria. "It wasn't me. She killed him, and planned to blackmail me to keep me from turning her in."

Before any of us could react, Gloria, her hands like claws, flew at Dominique. Dad lunged and caught Gloria by the wrists before she raked Dominique's face. Gloria screamed, "Why didn't you listen to me? But nooo! You had this whole 'let's confess' theory. 'We'll make ourselves look innocent,' you said. You stupid bitch!"

When Dad motioned, Tiny stood to his imposing six-foot-seven height. He said, "Ladies, you have the right to remain silent…" He continued reading Dominique and Gloria their rights as he escorted them to separate jail cells.

I silenced the speaker and spoke to Kellyanne. "I'm sorry about the baby."

A sob hitched her voice. "My gramma always says things happen for a reason, even when we're not wise enough to understand it."

"Your grandmother sounds like a very wise woman. What are your plans?"

Kellyanne sighed. "Cody was a good man. He'd just lost his way. I received a check from his lawyer with a letter stating that in Cody's will he had no known living relatives, and no liquid assets, but he had a safety deposit box. Tullah, the check was for fifty thousand dollars."

I couldn't help smiling. "How are you, really?"

"Better than I expected. I've been accepted to nursing school and plan to get my bachelor of science degree as an RN." There was a pause. "What will happen to Dominique and Gloria?"

"That's up to a judge and jury."

Epilogue

It took almost a year for the case to go to trial.

I turned on the television. There we were, standing on the courthouse steps. Dad stood tall and handsome in his tan cowboy hat, me at his side. We'd made the news. The reporter was giving an account of Cody's murder, and giving Dad and me credit for cracking a presumably unsolvable case.

I flicked the remote control to off.

Because the murder had taken place in Kentucky, Dominique aka Nikki Lewiki and Gloria Farnham were tried in a court of law in Louisville. A jury had found both women guilty of premeditated murder in the first degree.

Dominique tried to pull the temporary insanity card. I suppose she had seen too many movies and was trying to act her way out of a harsh sentence. Unfortunately, she would win no Oscars for her performance.

Kentucky still practices capital punishment. However, the jury considered all the evidence and the circumstances that led up to the murder and recommended leniency. The judge took that into his deliberations and sentenced Dominique and Gloria to life in prison.

The last I heard from Kellyanne, she had graduated and was working at Minnetonka General. She said she felt like she was slowly getting her life back, although, sadly, her beloved gramma had passed away peacefully.

That night, everyone that meant the world to me gathered at my house for a covered dish supper. During the meal, we hashed and rehashed the trial. We talked about the tragedy of Cody West's life, and that sometimes living behind prison walls for eternity might just as well be a death penalty for women like Dominique and Gloria.

Dad had already begun interviewing graduates from the police academy and veteran law officers desiring to leave big city crime for a smaller town and less violence.

Afterward, we gathered in the living room. I turned on the television and tuned in the western channel. We watched an old Roy Rogers cowboy movie. At the end, his magnificent palomino stallion reared and pawed the air. Roy doffed his white Stetson, smiled and said, "Adios, friends."

A part of me was sad that Cody West never conquered his fear of horses, and since he'd squandered his life, he didn't get to ride off into the sunset smiling.

We watched the movie credits until "The End" marched across the screen.

ENJOY ANOTHER SUSPENSEFUL
DOC HOLLIDAY MYSTERY

Loretta C. Rogers
Presents a Preview of

Monster in the Dark!

Prologue

She clapped her hands over her ears to shut out the voices. Ritual, they told her, was important. This was her first kill. Three, they said, was the magic number. Use a jigsaw, they said. Her hand trembled as she made the first cut. Blood splattered. She wiped the plastic face shield as best she could and kept at it. There was no stopping now.

She was sick of being told what to do. Sick of other people's expectations of her. Sick of the punishment. She mopped up the blood, leaving the room spotless. There was one little spot of red on the cuff that she had trouble getting out. Fearing punishment, she worried at the spot for a moment.

The voices scolded her. *You're late; you're late, for a very important date!*

She hissed, "Stop pestering me."

She finished dressing the corpse. And wouldn't all those people dressed in their Halloween costumes be surprised.

Because mine are the best costumes of all.

Chapter One

Something dreadful was going to happen. I knew this because when I woke up that morning I smelled blood. But I'm getting ahead of myself.

Friday night, and the townspeople had gathered to celebrate our annual three nights of Shocktober Fest. Revelers were enjoying the costumed Monster Mash barn dance. Enigma, Kentucky, was a dying town until my grandmother, Mayor Tanti Crow, and her friend, Vice Mayor Patty Sweet, courted a soft drink company to build their newest bottling plant in Enigma.

Sometimes growth of a rural town isn't good. Personally, I liked Enigma when it was a quaint community where everyone knew everyone else. Growth brings change, and most often that change comes in the form of more crime.

Tonight was the perfect setting for Halloween festivities. There was a chill in the air, a brisk breeze, and a full moon.

My name is Tullah Crow Holliday. Most everyone calls me Doc Holliday. I am a veterinarian and on occasion assist the sheriff with complicated cases. By the way, the sheriff is my father, John Henry Holliday, and before you ask, yes, our ancestor is the infamous outlaw better known as Doc Holliday.

If you're wondering why I, an animal doctor, assist my dad, it's because I was born with a special gift. It's not really a gift. It's a curse, a nuisance, one that quite often interferes with my life. I sense and feel and sometimes see things that are not visible to other people. I have a special connection with spirit animals. My mother and my grandmother were born in the *A-ni-wa-ya* (Wolf) clan. Tanti says it is because of my Cherokee heritage that I have these special abilities.

Tonight the large barn at the 4-H fairgrounds was decorated with pumpkins, scarecrows, and spider webs. The sounds of rattling chains, eerie moans, and cackles were piped through a sound system. People sat on bales of hay, enjoying a variety of refreshments. Normally, I'd rather eat sardines than dress up, especially in costume. To appease my grandmother, I had dressed as a jockey wearing red, white, and blue silks; after all, we do live in the great state known for horse racing.

My gaze lingered on the crowd. Patty Sweet was dressed as a giant donut. Maybe that's because she owns Sweets 'n' Eats café and pastry shop. Grandmother and our favorite curmudgeon, Dr. Paul Ritter, were dressed as Alice in Wonderland and Prince Charming. Even my ever so serious father had finally relented and dressed as his famous ancestor, John Henry "Doc" Holliday, complete with a fake handlebar mustache and dual pearl-handled pistols.

An eerie feeling had again crept over me. I shifted to my right, where a lone figure dressed as Little Red Riding Hood stood gazing at the crowd, her face obscured by the hood. Although she was a considerable distance from me, I could see from the stiff stance and fisted gloves that she was not happy.

"What bothers you, Little Sister? You have a troubled look in your eyes."

I forgot about Little Red Riding Hood and smiled up at my godfather, Charlie Whitehorse, who by the way was dressed as Paul Bunyan, which was quite appropriate since Charlie is a giant of a man. "I'm not sure, Uncle Charlie."

He wrapped my hand in his. "The band is finally playing a slow song. How 'bout a turn around the floor with an old man?"

I laughed and allowed him to lead me onto the dance floor, but then I shivered.

"There is a definite chill in the air. Are you cold?"

I shook my head and lowered my voice. "When I awoke this morning, I smelled blood."

"That is a bad omen, Little Sister."

He twirled me around the floor. I stopped and stood still. "Do you hear it, Uncle Charlie?"

"Hear what?"

"Horse's hooves. The horse is frightened. He's running."

Charlie tried to make light of my unease. "Aho, probably some rancher's thoroughbred jumped a fence and decided to join the party."

I didn't want to seem dramatic and decided not to say anything more.

In the middle of our dance, a gust of cold wind blew through the wide-open barn doors. A Friesian black stallion raced in from the darkness, his rider's black cape flapping in the wind. The stallion screamed and reared. It reared again and again. The rider on its back listed sideways, unable to control the frightened animal.

The band stopped playing. People scattered to avoid the frantic horse's dangerous hooves. Parents gathered their screaming children.

I raced forward and held out my hand. I spoke to the frightened horse in the language of my mother's ancestors.

The stallion tossed its magnificent head and pawed the floor. I could almost see my reflection in the large black eyes. I inched forward and continued speaking until I got close enough to grab the dangling reins.

Someone from the crowd shouted, "Look, it's the headless horseman! He definitely wins the contest for most authentic costume."

Nervous laughter filtered around the room. One of the band members blew his bugle. The blast caused the mighty horse to rear, lifting me off my feet. I grabbed the bridle's cheek straps and held on.

Uncle Charlie rushed to my aid. The frightened animal fought against the restraint, and then the unspeakable happened. The rider tumbled from the saddle and crashed to the floor.

Folks twittered and pointed, like a joke had just happened. I've always wondered why people laugh when they witness someone getting hurt. By this time, Dad was at my side. My stomach roiled. Don't get me wrong, I'm used to seeing blood and guts and gore—though it's not exactly an image I want rattling around inside my brain. This, however, was an exception. The metallic odor of blood fouled my nose.

"Dad, someone has chopped off his head."

"Who is the victim supposed to be?"

"Brom Bones Van Brunt, a character from the fairy tale *The Legend of Sleepy Hollow*." I noticed the only thing missing from the costume was a carved jack-o'-lantern.

A note was pinned to the dead person's jacket. I say "person" because at this point we weren't sure if the corpse was a man or a woman.

I reached for the piece of paper. Dad stopped me.

Deputy Tiny Goodbody knelt beside us. "Figured you could use these." He pulled a pair of evidence gloves from the pocket of his jacket and handed them over.

Dad thanked him. "Tiny, clear the room. I'm afraid the party's over."

Uncle Charlie led the horse outside. I stood to follow, but Dad said, "Tullah, I need you here."

I nodded and remained next to the body. There was something about this scenario that didn't sit right with me.

Dad unpinned the note and read aloud, "I am death, and I make all people equal." It was signed "Godfather of Death."

"Dad, that's a quote from the Brothers Grimm fairy tales."

"You're frowning. What's bothering you, Tullah?"

"Nothing."

"That's not your *nothing* face."

"Okay, two things." I pointed. "Except for that small speck on the cuff, there's no blood."

"Yeah, and what's number two?"

Dad's expression flattened when I said, "Where's the head?"

He stared at me for a moment, his blue eyes growing dark and tension suddenly lining his face. "Tullah, I'm going to need you on this one. It appears we have a real sicko running loose."

Don't miss any of the suspenseful installments in

Loretta C. Rogers' bestselling series featuring

Veterinarian Dr. Tullah Holliday,

who uses her empathic abilities to solve crimes.

A word about the author…

A native Floridian and proud of her Scots-Irish heritage, Loretta C. Rogers is a bestselling author. Her books are in libraries throughout the USA and Europe. She lives in Florida with her husband and dog.

Thank You!
If you enjoyed *Lights…Camera…Murder!*, your review is highly appreciated.

https://amzn.to/2GBb0iI

Thank you for purchasing
this publication of The Wild Rose Press, Inc.

For questions or more information
contact us at
info@thewildrosepress.com.

The Wild Rose Press, Inc.

www.ingramcontent.com/pod-product-compliance
Lightning Source LLC
Chambersburg PA
CBHW060552260626
47161CB00003B/1163